"This is where I want to be."

As he pulled her up to him and lifted her off her feet, Lexie felt as if they'd been together every day of the past thirteen years. "And this is where I feel safe," she replied, trying to erase the memory of the fear she'd tasted barely an hour before. She touched the scar on Simon's chest, wondering if he ever really felt safe anymore.

They held each other, until finally he kissed her open-mouthed, and it didn't take her long to find the frenzy he sought. They made love as if it might be the last time.

Which indeed it might, Lexie thought, wrapping her arms around his neck and holding on as if she'd never let him go.

The gunman or another thug for hire could get to them. Or Simon could simply realize he'd made a mistake in coming back to Jenkins Cove and take off for parts unknown.

This might be the last night she'd have with the man she loved—a reason to make it memorable enough to last a lifetime.

PATRICIA ROSEMOOR

CHRISTMAS DELIVERY

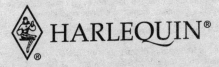 HARLEQUIN®

TORONTO • NEW YORK • LONDON
AMSTERDAM • PARIS • SYDNEY • HAMBURG
STOCKHOLM • ATHENS • TOKYO • MILAN • MADRID
PRAGUE • WARSAW • BUDAPEST • AUCKLAND

Since the theme of *Christmas Delivery* has to do with getting justice for the evil that is done to others, I would like to dedicate the book to the relentless Task Force that, after three years, identified and arrested my father's murderer using DNA evidence.

ISBN-13: 978-0-373-88875-7
ISBN-10: 0-373-88875-9

CHRISTMAS DELIVERY

Copyright © 2008 by Patricia Pinianski

www.eHarlequin.com

Printed in U.S.A.

ABOUT THE AUTHOR

Patricia Rosemoor has always had a fascination with dangerous love. She loves bringing a mix of thrills and chills and romance to Harelquin Intrigue readers. She's won a Golden Heart from Romance Writers of America and Reviewers' Choice and Career Achievement Awards from *Romantic Times BOOKreviews*. She teaches Writing Popular Fiction and Suspense-Thriller Writing in the Fiction Writing department of Columbia College Chicago. Check out her Web site, www.PatriciaRosemoor.com. You can contact Patricia either via e-mail at Patricia@PatriciaRosemoor.com, or through the publisher, c/o Harlequin/Silhouette Books, 233 Broadway, New York, NY 10279.

Books by Patricia Rosemoor

HARLEQUIN INTRIGUE
707—VIP PROTECTOR**
745—THE BOYS IN BLUE
     "Zachary"
785—VELVET ROPES**
791—ON THE LIST**
858—GHOST HORSE
881—RED CARPET CHRISTMAS**
924—SLATER HOUSE
958—TRIGGERED RESPONSE
1031—WOLF MOON*
1047—IN NAME ONLY?*
1101—CHRISTMAS DELIVERY

*The McKenna Legacy
**Club Undercover

CAST OF CHARACTERS

Lexie Thornton—When the landscape designer realizes she's not seeing the ghost of her daughter's father, she tries to protect both her daughter and herself from heartbreak.

Simon Shea—The ex-mercenary comes back from the "dead" to expose the secrets of Jenkins Cove and reclaim the woman he's always loved.

Clifford Drake—Does the charming playboy have a darker side?

Police Chief Charles Hammer—Is he lazy—or hiding something?

Ned Perry—The land developer acts like he'd *kill* to get his hands on prime real estate.

Phil Cardon—Who does the handyman really work for?

Isabella Faust—Is the maid really infatuated with Cliff, or does she have other reasons to stay close to the Drakes?

Doug Heller—The manager of Drake Enterprises seems to have his hand in everything that goes on in Jenkins Cove.

Prologue

Christmas Eve, thirteen years ago

Wind howled along the Chesapeake and drove a stinging wall of snow at Simon Shea, virtually blinding him. Somehow he made it off the road and into the woods, where the unusually fierce winter storm abated some. Dropping his duffel bag, he stopped for a moment and leaned against the trunk of a pine to catch his breath. He could hardly move, could hardly think, what with weather conditions that threatened to ruin his carefully made plans.

Even in the woods, the wind haunted him, moaning and rattling ice-covered tree branches overhead. Geared up to get free of Jenkins Cove— to get away from his drunk of a father, from his cold, bitter life—he had to do it tonight.

Thank God, Lexie was coming with him.

That's all Simon had been thinking about since convincing her to run the night before, as they lay together, snug in their wooded shelter, his angular body protectively wrapped around her soft one. Being with her…starting a new life together… waking up happy with her in his arms every morning for the rest of their lives—they were the best Christmas presents in the world!

She'd hesitated at first and he'd understood her arguments. They were awfully young to go off on their own. She hadn't finished high school yet. And what about college? But Simon had sworn that he would protect her and provide for her and find a way for her to do everything she ever wanted. She'd smiled at him then—that crooked, heart-wrenching, only-for-him smile that had made him fall for her in the first place—and he'd known everything was going to be all right.

He'd better get going. Didn't want to be late. Didn't want to scare Lexie into thinking he'd gotten cold feet. They were to meet behind the church at half-past midnight to start their new life together on Christmas morning.

Picking up the duffel bag, he decided to stay off the main road and take the shortcut through the woods into town. Luckily, he knew those woods like the back of his hand. Every path, every detour around danger. There were a couple of swampy areas the locals stayed away from. They could trap a man, suck him down and bury him alive. Not much different than living with Rufus Shea, Simon thought, fighting guilt that he was leaving his old man alone. He just couldn't take it anymore— couldn't take being caregiver to a drunk who'd given up—not when he could start a decent life with Lexie.

Simon was so engrossed in thoughts of their future, that at first he didn't hear the approaching sounds until they exploded through the trees.

A series of shouts raised the short hairs on the back of his neck and made his pulse jag. He stopped dead in his tracks. What the hell was going on?

He looked around in confusion, caught blurred movement through the trees and zeroed in on a kid flying through the woods as if his life depended on it.

Another teenager, younger than him, Simon thought, heart thumping against his ribs now. Snow dusted the mop of curly pale hair. The kid wasn't dressed for the cold; he had on only a thin leather jacket and ripped jeans. He was no one Simon recognized.

Still, something made him call out to the terrified kid. "Hey! You need help?"

But the kid threw a fast, panicked look behind him and kept running until a whine shattered the quiet. Then he led with his chest, head and arms flung back as his body snapped into an impossible arch before he fell first to his knees, then face forward onto the snow-covered ground.

Not knowing whether he should see if he could help the kid or run for town, Simon hesitated a moment. His mistake.

Chapter One

Turning the Drake House ballroom into a winter wonderland for the annual Christmas charity ball should make her happier, Lexie Thornton thought. The main room in the west wing was two stories high, with a balcony off the second-floor parlors, and nearly one hundred feet long, fifty wide. Doors with glass insets lined one wall, leading to an outside balcony with a view of the gardens and the Chesapeake Bay beyond. Decorating the mansion for the ball was quite a feat and would take several days to complete.

Lexie pushed up the sleeves of her sweater, looked around the ballroom, then glanced down to her laptop to review the design she'd planned out.

"Hey, Lexie, where do we put these?"

She looked up to see two of her garden shop workers hauling in large poinsettia plants, each planter encased in red or green foil and wrapped with a huge gold bow. "Just set them in an area free of drafts for now."

Today would be devoted to the basics—dividing the ballroom with its gleaming wood floors and trim into several distinct areas for dancing and socializing over drinks and displaying the silent auction items. Virtually the whole town of Jenkins Cove would show up for the ball, and Lexie would make the most of every inch of available space.

That she would be responsible for giving so many people pleasure didn't bring a smile to her face. Ironic that Christmas was so important to Thornton Garden Center, the family business that she now ran. Her parents both still worked there, but in more relaxed capacities. They were both retirement age, but refused to retire, saying it would make them feel old. Decorating public areas as well as private estates and businesses for Christmas brought in a solid portion of the year's income, so Lexie couldn't hide from the holiday.

Call her the Christmas Grinch, especially since the ball and the silent auction would raise money for the Drake Foundation, which supported several local charities. This included one that helped impoverished single mothers and their children—a cause dear to Lexie's heart, since she was a single mother herself.

Frowning at the further reminder of why Christmas always made her so sad, she looked for her best friend.

Marie Leonard stood in front of the fireplace, the

focal point of the room, and stared into the large, antique mirror hanging over the mantel. When she turned away from the mirror, her expression went beyond happy—she was glowing, actually, so that the color in her cheeks intensified the chestnut color of her hair. For the first time since she'd returned to Jenkins Cove after her father's death, Marie seemed at peace.

Lexie was happy for her dear friend, who was about to start a new life. Marie was madly in love with Brandon Drake, owner of this estate, and their engagement was to be officially announced at the ball. Which Lexie would be forced to attend, making her relive her loss all over again.

Christmas Eve…

Thirteen years and she wasn't over the heartbreak.

Thirteen years ago, instead of meeting her behind the church as planned, Simon had gotten himself killed in an accident taking the shortcut through the woods. Even after all this time, thinking about it brought a lump to her throat and a tightness in her chest.

"Hey, those are gorgeous plants," Marie said, crossing to her.

"Thanks. Gorgeous plants for a gorgeous room."

Though Lexie tried to inject enthusiasm into her voice, she knew she failed when Marie gave her that look that told her if she wanted to talk, Marie was there for her. Not that Lexie was planning to take her friend up on that. She didn't want to talk about Simon anymore, didn't want to think about him, didn't want to remember…only, considering the circumstances, how could she ever forget?

Before Marie could try to force the conversation, noise from the foyer had the other woman turning toward the entry. "Ah, the caterer has arrived. I need to talk to her, see what final selections she made for the buffet." She moved in that direction, glancing back at Lexie to say, "But don't imagine *you're* home free."

Lexie groaned at her friend's implied threat. Then she got back to work, referring to the checklist and the decorating design on her laptop to see where she was.

Dozens of poinsettias had been brought in. Hopefully, she'd planned enough plants and greenery for the ballroom to help improve the air quality. The fire that had damaged the east wing of Drake House had left a thick stench that was difficult to mask, despite the clean-up efforts of a professional crew. Later, she would add dozens of pots of mums and gerbera daisies to the decor—both would help purify the air.

The first order of business was to distribute the poinsettias the way she'd mapped them out in the room. So she spent the next hour with her landscape workers, making sure every plant was in its proper place. Then she had her workers fetch the mantel swag and the garlands that would be hung around every door—a time-consuming job, but one that would help transform the old mansion for the season.

A familiar laugh echoed from the entranceway. Lexie went to investigate the foyer, where the master staircase split upward to each wing. Well, one wing now. The private wing was unlivable because part of the roof had collapsed during a fire, so it was cordoned off and would be for some time to come. Marie and Brandon were occupying rooms in the public wing and the servants were all housed off grounds.

In the foyer, Lexie found Marie with Chelsea Caldwell, looking soft and lovely in a white cashmere sweater and matching beret, and her fiancé, Michael Bryant.

"For the silent auction," the blonde said, handing Marie a painting.

"Oh, nice." Marie waved Lexie over.

A quick look and Lexie's brows shot up. Chelsea had painted a view of Jenkins Creek. While water was a good part of the canvas, the focus was the dueling estates perched on points that faced each other—Drake House on one side and the Manor at Drake Acres on the other. Brandon had inherited the older estate from his father, Jonathan. Always competitive, his uncle Cliff, the younger of the brothers, had built what he'd considered a bigger and better estate.

"Hmm, I have a feeling I know who will be bidding against each other on this item." Knowing Cliff, Lexie thought he would pay any amount to keep the piece from his nephew.

"That was the idea," Chelsea admitted. "More money for charity."

"You would have had bidders competing against each other no matter which painting you donated," Michael murmured, pulling her closer.

Chelsea blushed and grinned and Lexie noted the diamond ring on the other woman's left hand. So the engagement was official. Lexie quickly looked away.

"Rumor has it you have a new book contract," Marie said to Michael.

But it was Chelsea who enthusiastically said, "Michael is going to write a fictional account of the human trafficking that went on here for decades."

"All names changed to protect the innocent," Michael promised.

"Congratulations," Lexie said, zeroing her attention onto one of her workers waving to her. "I need to get back to work. I'll see you both at the ball."

Seeing how right Chelsea and Michael were for each other, as were Brandon and Marie, Lexie felt a sharp pang of longing. Would *she* ever find someone to love, to share things with again?

Would she ever have a second chance at a real life?

IT WAS THAT IDEA of wanting a second chance that finally convinced Lexie to accept Marie's dare to try the psychomanteum at the House of Seven Gables, the bed-and-breakfast run by Chelsea's aunt, Sophie Caldwell. Marie had tried to push Lexie into doing it before, but pragmatic Lexie had resisted.

Since she'd ridden out to Drake House in one of the garden center's trucks with her workers, Marie drove her into town. They left the car in the parking lot near the church and walked the short distance to the B&B, which was situated on the harbor.

"I just wish you the same happiness I rediscovered with Brandon." The sun had set and Marie pulled her wool coat closer. "I never thought it would happen, but it did. Who's to say it can't happen for you? You just have to learn to let go."

"Katie is my life."

"I didn't mean let go of *her*, just…"

"I know. But every time I look into her eyes, I see Simon. Maybe I'm not meant to be with anyone else."

Maybe that's why her life consisted of running the family business and raising her twelve-year-old daughter. Period. No time off for good behavior.

"Or maybe you've just decided to protect yourself against potential loss," Marie said. "You don't know what will happen in that room. Maybe you'll learn the truth about what happened to Simon. Isn't that worth the risk? The truth can give you peace. And then you can move on. You can't protect yourself from love forever, Lexie. Love is a *good* thing. Simon wouldn't want you to be alone. He would want you to find someone to fulfill you as a woman, as well as a mother."

Lexie sighed. "Now you're romanticizing."

"You could *use* a little romanticizing. If only you could commune with Simon, perhaps you could let him go, move on to someone new. It's more than time, Lexie."

"When you're right, you're right."

No use arguing with Marie when she got an idea into her head.

Lexie figured that giving in to her friend's insistence that she visit the psychomanteum was romantic enough for anyone. Basically, she'd agreed in order to get Marie to stop fretting over her. And, she had to admit, there was something else.

Even though she wasn't a believer, a little part of her wished she could see Simon one last time….

They circled the House of the Seven Gables with its long, two-story porch. The bed-and-breakfast faced the harbor and was situated directly across from a seafood restaurant, a prime stopping place for tourists who came to sail or take boat rides to see the waterfront estates.

As they turned the corner, the wind whipped up with an odd wail and Lexie pulled the front of her brown suede Sherpa jacket closed against the chill. The wind out of nowhere and the late afternoon mist coming off the water seemed to be omens of some kind.

Either that or her imagination was working overtime.

The long building of white clapboard had dormer windows under the gabled roof. Lexie quickly took the steps up to the front door, Marie following. The Christmas wreath hanging there was decorated with miniature duck decoys, small sailboats and Maryland crabs. Lexie couldn't take credit for the unusual holiday decor. Sophie Caldwell had her own unique ideas.

Like the psychomanteum.

"Ah, there you are," Sophie said when they entered the hall.

Just coming out of the office, the owner of the B&B retied the lace-trimmed apron covering her dark skirt. Attached to her green blouse was a pin as striking as the porch decorations—Rudolph the reindeer, his red nose blinking on and off. As usual, her graying blond hair was pulled into a neat bun at the nape of her neck, and a gentle smile played over her lips.

"Sorry we're late," Marie said. "But Chelsea stopped by with her painting for the auction, and I guess we lost track of time."

At the mention of her niece, Sophie beamed. "Is

that all?" She looked to Lexie. "I was afraid that you'd changed your mind."

"Hard to do when someone's twisting your arm behind your back," Lexie muttered.

Sophie checked Lexie's arm as if expecting to see it in Marie's grasp. Then she shook her head and said, "Can I get you girls something? Tea and some fresh cookies?"

"Oh, no, not for me." A spiraling sensation Lexie defined as pure fear shot through her, making her stomach cramp at the thought of food. "Just the…um…"

"Upstairs," Sophie said kindly, then turned to Marie. "While you wait, you and I can have a nice catch-up in the kitchen, dear."

"Sure," Marie said, though she was staring at Lexie as if for a cue.

"Go." Lexie shushed her off and headed for the stairs. "I need to do this alone anyway."

Before she could talk herself out of it, Lexie proceeded up to the third floor and headed down the hallway, stopping only in front of the door to the psychomanteum. This was just plain silly. A pragmatic person, Lexie didn't succumb to flights of fancy. Why, then, did she feel as if her limbs were made of lead?

Taking a deep breath, she opened the door and stepped into the room whose ceiling was painted black and whose walls were hung with black curtains. Her heart was beating double time and her stomach was knotting as she looked around. A chair in the middle of the room faced an ornately framed mirror that leaned against a wall. Chests and small tables around the room held candles of various sizes. Lexie dimmed the ceiling fixture and the room immediately became spookier.

Her legs felt like rubber as she moved to the chair and sat facing the mirror.

Now what?

She supposed she should light the candles, but it was as if something had a grip on her and she couldn't move. The back of her neck prickled and her breath came harsh and she had to force it through stiff lips.

Stop it… This is silly!

It was. Really. And yet she couldn't make herself leave. She sat there, frozen, staring into the mirror. She let her own image go out of focus and instead thought of Simon as she had last seen him—tall and rangy, shaggy light brown hair framing a rugged face and heavy-lidded deep green eyes.

"Simon, why did you have to die?" she whispered, her stomach churning. "Why did you have to leave me?"

Questions she'd asked the ether over and over again through the years, especially when she'd learned that she was pregnant and again after having a baby she'd vowed to raise on her own.

She got no answers. Not then. Not now.

She concentrated harder.

Remembered the first time Simon had pulled her braids and teased her when she was six.

Remembered the first time he'd pushed a bully away from her when she was eleven.

Remembered the first time he'd kissed her when she was fifteen.

So many memories, each one treasured, never to be forgotten, all to be taken out and examined at will, usually when the loneliness got to her. Times when she found it hard to believe he was dead at all. Surely part of her would have died with him!

She'd never felt lonelier than now, when her vow was to leave all those memories behind and go on. To make new ones. Maybe to meet someone she could love who wasn't Simon Shea.

Could she do it?

"Simon, if you can…if it's possible…come back to me now, even if only for a moment. Assure me that I can trust the future. Let me say goodbye properly."

Not just by spilling tears over his grave.

For years, she'd dreamed of Simon. Dreamed of the first and only time they'd slept together. Dreamed that they'd run away together as they'd planned. Dreamed that he wasn't dead at all, but was by her side, raising their daughter.

Dreamed that she was happy when she was anything but.

Could she abandon her dream world to the real one and trust that if she found someone new to love he wouldn't leave her alone and brokenhearted as Simon had? Could Simon reassure her that wouldn't happen?

No matter how hard she tried to see her ghostly love in the mirror, no matter how much she needed to do so, Lexie simply couldn't.

Her anxiety receded.

Her stomach leveled.

Her heart slowed to a normal beat.

"Goodbye, then," she whispered and left the room.

She raced downstairs to the kitchen where Marie and Sophie were laughing and scooping cookies off metal baking sheets. They looked up and when Marie's gaze met Lexie's, her expression fell. "No luck?" she asked.

Lexie shook her head. "Thanks anyway, Sophie." To Marie she said, "I need to get home, so I'll see you tomorrow."

"Wait, I'll drive you."

"No need. I could use a run."

Lexie was already backpedaling out of the kitchen. She practically ran from the B&B out into a pea-soup fog. Slowing, she felt for the stairs, then once on solid ground picked up her pace once more.

She hadn't been kidding about needing a run—she felt as if she were being chased by memories—but took it slower than she might have because of the fog. The boots she wore were practical for her work, but not for running. Jogging parallel to town, she waited until she could steer clear of the shops and anyone she knew and then crossed over to the other side.

Avoiding Thornton Garden Center and any employees still around who might detain her, she zigzagged the few blocks to a gravel road that fronted a couple of properties, including her own. The house was closer to the water than the road.

Taking the shortcut through the woods, Lexie once more got that weird feeling she'd had when forcing herself into the psychomanteum. Her pulse was racing and her stomach cramping.

Man, she'd really spooked herself! There was no reason to fear crossing through the familiar woods.

So why did she?

The pines seemed to close in on her and the wind whistled a message she couldn't understand.

A warning?

Weird things had been going on in Jenkins Cove, but not around here. And they were over. The criminals were dead or behind bars.

So why did she get the distinct feeling that danger lurked right around the corner?

"Thank you, Marie," she muttered. Her friend had opened her to unrealistic expectations. It was her own fault that she was turning them into something else.

Slowing to a stop, she stooped over to catch her breath. And regain her sanity. She took a moment to look around, peer deep into the surrounding fog.

There was nothing threatening her other than her own imagination.

No danger.

No nothing.

Or was there?

A rustle was followed by ghostly movement deep in the woods.

A deer, Lexie told herself. Just a deer.

Even so, she backed off, toward the house, her gaze pinned to the very spot through the trees where she'd seen something…

Only when she was just about there did the fog shift for a moment.

And for a moment—just that moment she had wished for—Simon Shea stared back at her.

Chapter Two

Simon pulled back, making himself invisible a moment too late. An expert tactical fighter, he should have known better than to expose himself like that.

He'd simply wanted to get closer.

With senses honed sharper than the average person's, he watched her ghostlike figure through the fog as she gazed around, seeming alarmed. And confused. She continued on her way, faster now, every so often glancing over her shoulder as if her nerves had gotten the better of her. As if she were expecting to see him there, behind her.

But was it *him* that she'd seen?

Had she actually recognized him?

Doubtful, he thought. He wasn't the boy who'd left Jenkins Cove all those years ago. He'd matured. Had bulked up. Had grown harder. Though the last wasn't necessarily something she would notice, at least not at a distance. But both time and a life working as a mercenary had changed him.

He might have grown harder—a requisite for his survival—but the moment he'd spotted Lexie coming from the dock area, Simon had known he still had a soft spot for the girl he'd been forced to abandon. He'd recognized her tall, graceful form immediately, and a closer look made him feel as if time had stood still. Her dark hair was as long and as thick as ever, her skin as pale and smooth, her gray eyes as large and inviting. And though she wore a sheepskin jacket, he had a sense of familiar curves more lush than ever.

Wanting to know more about the woman Lexie Thornton had become, Simon hadn't been able to stop himself from following her.

He hadn't meant to scare her, but of course he had. Too familiar with the vibes put out by fear— mostly people who'd feared *him*—he could sense what Lexie was feeling and therefore was extra careful not to repeat his mistake.

He didn't want her to know he was here in town, at least not yet.

He didn't want anyone in Jenkins Cove to know.

Until he learned the truth about what had happened to him thirteen years ago, he wanted to remain a ghost.

Only after seeing the news flash about a mass grave found a couple of miles outside of the town proper—and that those buried there had had their organs harvested—did he realize that he had to return to Maryland and learn how he'd ended up in some third world country bearing arms. He'd been a victim of human trafficking as much as any of the victims in that grave. The only difference was that he was still alive.

At least his body was.

Before the media had its field day with the story, he'd been wandering the States, aimless, having freed himself at last from the company that had controlled his life for so long. Employment as a soldier in a private army had its financial rewards, however, and when he'd left, he'd had more money than he'd needed.

What he hadn't had was a life.

Not that he'd come here to reclaim his. Simon knew it was too late for that. In more than a decade working for Shadow Ops, a private military company hired by the CIA to run "peacekeeping" operations in third world countries, he'd done things he'd never imagined doing. Like the time a month into his enforced service when, after delivering medical supplies to a village in Somalia, he'd been surrounded by an angry mob. He'd thought he could bluff his way past them and back to his unit, until he'd been caught from behind and a man with a knife came at him. If he hadn't reacted fast, Simon would have been stabbed to death.

In the end, the assailant lay dead, the one who'd held him wounded. Afterward he didn't even remember what had happened. It was only much later that he'd reacted to his first kill.

He'd been brought to his knees, his stomach emptying.

The dead man's ghost had haunted him day and night for months afterward.

Eventually, Simon had hardened himself against the reality of war, the only way he could deal with it, since violence had quickly become a way of life.

Just because he finally freed himself of that life didn't cleanse him of what he'd been forced to do. He couldn't escape his past, and he wouldn't wish himself on any other human being, certainly not on a woman he'd once loved.

His jaw tightened at his reaction to seeing Lexie again.

She reached a house set in a semicircular stand of pines. It was a neat two-story with an upper deck overlooking the woods. Did she get to the deck from her bedroom? Suddenly imagining himself on the bed there with her, Simon cursed. What was he thinking? She was probably married with a couple of kids. No room for someone like him in her life.

Unlocking the front door, Lexie stepped halfway inside before turning again to look his way. Even protected by the deepening woods and fog, Simon slid behind a tree and leaned his back against it. He closed his eyes for a moment and cursed himself for following her.

Now Lexie would be afraid because of him.

He'd never meant for that to happen.

He simply hadn't been able to help himself. He'd had to follow her, would have to learn everything he could about her and her life.

His mistake.

Again.

Because now Simon knew something irrefutable, something that would only bring him more misery, more heartache, something he didn't want to admit, didn't want to think about.

Thirteen years might as well have been thirteen days.

He was still in love with Lexie Thornton.

WEIRDED OUT thinking she'd seen Simon, Lexie hovered around the door and every few seconds looked out the window. But if anyone had truly been out there, he was gone now.

What had she really seen?

Nothing had happened in the psychomanteum, but what if the effects had followed her and once she'd relaxed…

Had she really seen Simon's ghost?

Was it possible?

Or was her mind playing tricks on her because she'd been thinking about him so intently?

She closed her eyes and replayed the moment in her mind. The Simon she had seen had been tall, but not rangy. He'd had light brown hair, but it was short and spiked, not shaggy and unkempt. His features had been familiar and yet not. They'd been older, mature, more rugged. They'd seemed closed and hard, especially his mouth, which had been set in a straight line.

The one thing that had been the same—exactly the same—had been his eyes. She'd been too far away to see the color, but they'd been heavy-lidded, incredibly sexy.

Simon's eyes had been the first thing that had attracted her to him. They'd held a promise that he had indeed kept. They were eyes that haunted her dreams. And her waking hours.

So what had she seen? A ghost?

If so, this ghost was of a man her age, not a teenager.

More than likely, her imagination had been playing tricks on her, creating what she'd wanted to see most.

Or…what if it had been a real man following her and her imagination had turned him into a mature Simon?

That set her heart to racing and she looked more intently toward the tree line, fearing she might see some stalker watching the house, waiting for her to leave again.

"Hey, Mom, what's up? Is something out there?"

Starting, heart pounding, Lexie turned to find Katie coming down the stairs. Her daughter shared her own features—all except her eyes. "I don't know. Fog's too thick." She looked into Katie's green eyes—Simon's eyes—and lied. "I heard something before coming in. A deer or raccoon probably." No way was she going to share her thoughts with her daughter and scare the kid out of her wits.

"Oh." Athletic and wiry, curves only now starting to soften her hips and chest, Katie shrugged and bounced down the last few stairs. "What did you bring home for dinner?"

"Dinner? Oh, no, I forgot I said I'd pick something up." That she'd been too distracted with thoughts of Simon to remember made her feel awful. "I don't think there's anything in the freezer, either."

Katie groaned. "Canned soup and sandwiches again?"

"Sorry, sorry, sorry!"

"Other mothers cook."

"Other mothers don't run family businesses."

Katie heaved a sigh. "Fine. Your not cooking hasn't killed me yet."

Lexie put her arms around her daughter and kissed the top of her head. She had to rise up on her toes to do so these days. Though only twelve, Katie was nearly as tall as she was. Still freaked after thinking she had seen Simon, Lexie held on tight to his daughter. Too tight.

Squirming out of her arms with a "Mo-o-om!" Katie headed for the refrigerator.

Not only was her little girl not so little anymore, she was getting uncomfortable with big shows of affection. Lexie sighed, knowing their relationship was bound to change as Katie matured. Lexie understood that, understood that she would have to loosen the reins.

She didn't have to like it.

She hung her jacket on the hall tree, kicked off her wet boots, slipped her feet into a pair of clogs she kept by the front door, then joined her daughter in the kitchen.

They worked together preparing the meal, smoothly as always. Lexie started the sandwiches, while Katie opened the can of soup and poured it into a pot on the stove.

The kitchen was old-fashioned—hickory cabinets, butcher block counters, big single porcelain sink, plank wood floors, old appliances—but Lexie liked it exactly as the last owners had left it, so she'd never even thought about updating. The only thing she'd done was paint the walls a deep gold and had the original window replaced with a garden window so she could grow fresh herbs all year round.

Even if she didn't have time to cook meals from scratch very often, the herbs looked pretty and smelled wonderful.

"Nana said she'd teach me to cook," Katie said, as if reading her mind.

"That's nice of her, but I don't want you to think it's your responsibility to make dinner."

"I'd just like to know how, in case I wanted to."

"Okay."

Katie was aware that her grandmother was the better cook by far. Lexie knew they would enjoy spending the extra time together.

"We're going to start with Christmas cookies tomorrow night."

"On Thursday? What about school on Friday? I remember how Mom gets carried away with her baking and doesn't know when to stop. You need your sleep."

"Nothing goes on in school the last day before the holiday but parties. Actually, Nana wants me to stay for a couple of nights so we can have a marathon cookie-making session. Don't worry. She'll make sure I get enough sleep. Aunt Carole's going to help, too, when she's not at the garden center."

Hardly a domestic goddess herself, Lexie wasn't surprised that no one had invited *her*. No doubt because her mother knew that if she went it would simply be to eat the cookies everyone else made, as she had done when she was a teenager.

Knowing she was going to be too busy finishing up the decorating for the charity ball to have time to spend with her daughter this weekend, Lexie said, "As long as you promise to bring tons of cookies home for me."

Katie grinned. "Deal."

Lexie smacked her lips in anticipation and set the sandwiches on the table.

Dinner, such as it was, allowed Lexie to spend precious time with Katie. Between her own work and Katie's school and activities with her friends, breakfast and dinner were the only times she could count on their being together during the school year. A top student, Katie would spend the rest of the evening holed up in her room doing homework. And, no doubt, e-mailing or text-messaging her friends.

But for half an hour, Lexie got the update on Katie's schoolwork, her activities, the other kids. She appreciated every precious moment.

"So when are we gonna go pick out a Christmas tree?" Katie asked.

"After I recover from the ball at Drake House."

Katie gave her a big sigh. "Cutting it close again. That means Christmas Eve."

"I know, sweetheart. I'm sorry. But you know how important this season is to the business."

"Someday I wish we could put up our decorations before you get so busy."

Lexie laughed. "You mean right after Halloween?"

"Why not?"

"We'd have to get a fake tree, then. A real one wouldn't last until New Year's."

"Might be worth it."

"If you want to do that next year, it's a done deal."

"Cool." Katie grinned at her and Lexie grinned back.

In reality, she knew Katie would change her mind when the time came. Picking out a real tree together and cutting it down themselves was a time-honored tradition they both loved. And Katie would purposely sleep on the couch some nights because she loved being surrounded by the pine scent. Even so, they could at least put up lights in the windows and do some other early decorating as a compromise.

Though Katie was finished eating, she sat there a while, as if she had something else on her mind.

Finally, she said, "So there's a Christmas party Saturday night, but Nana says I need your permission to go."

"Christmas party where? At school?"

"No. It's a private party. In a house."

"Whose house?"

"Josh Pearson's."

"Josh Pearson." Lexie tried to place him. "Have I met him? Has he been here?" She'd always encouraged Katie to invite her friends over, so that she would get to know who her daughter hung out with.

"Um, no."

"But he's in your class."

Katie bit her lip, then said, "No, he's in high school."

"How old is he?"

"Sixteen." Now Katie sounded truculent.

"Katie, you're twelve."

"I just want to go to a party—"

"For teenagers."

"So I'm a preteen."

A designation she'd given herself since she'd turned twelve.

"Even if you were thirteen I wouldn't let you go to a private party with high school kids," Lexie said. "You're only in seventh grade, for heaven's sake. Stop trying to grow up so fast!"

Katie jumped to her feet. "You just want to ruin my life!"

"Just for a little while longer," Lexie said, refusing to engage in a debate. "Please clear the table before you escape to your room."

Katie was clearly fighting tears as she did as ordered, then refused to say another word before rushing back upstairs.

Lexie sighed and shook her head. Her mother

had always said it would serve Lexie right to have a daughter just like her—and she had. Just as long as Katie didn't get pregnant at seventeen the way she had. The time for the safe-and-responsible-sex talk was coming up, but Lexie hoped to delay it just a little longer.

Thinking about it made her think of Simon again. She tried to watch television to distract herself, but she couldn't concentrate, no matter which program she tried. Her gaze was continually pulled to the front door.

Eventually she gave up the sham and got off the couch, grabbed her jacket from the hall tree and went outside.

Not that she planned to go anywhere.

On the porch, she stared out toward the path she'd taken through the woods.

What had she seen earlier?

Some version of Simon, but whether ghost or her imagination or some guy she put the wrong face to, she didn't know.

Even now, Lexie sensed something out there— ghost or man?—but no matter how hard she stared through the tree line, she saw nothing.

The damp cold got to her eventually, driving her back inside.

Unable to stop thinking of Simon, Lexie got ready for bed. She could hardly keep her eyes open, and when she climbed under the covers, her eyes drifted closed.

Even so, Simon's image stayed with her, fading only as she fell asleep….

He stood in the fog, staring at her as if silently calling her to him. Pulse fluttering, she moved closer, and when the fog swallowed him, she ran into the thick, wet air to catch up to him. She couldn't let him get away from her again!

Suddenly she was jerked off her feet. He caught her around the waist and spun her in his arms so that they were face-to-face. Breathless, she reached up and touched the features that were familiar and yet not.

"Simon?"

"I came back for you. I love you…always have…"

He kissed her then, and her heart swelled with happiness.

When he ran his hands down her sides and cupped her bottom and pulled her to him, she gasped with desire.

She held on tight…clung to him. She would never let him go again…

Chapter Three

Lexie drove her SUV to Drake House the next morning and told her workers to meet her there. Tired from a night of tossing and turning, and, yes, dreaming of Simon, she'd armed herself with an entire thermos of coffee.

She chugged down the last of a cup as she rode alongside the bay, noting a couple of boats slapping across the water even though it was past mid-December. She wondered why anyone would want to be out there in weather like this. In a few weeks, weather would force the owners to dock their boats for the rest of the winter.

When she pulled into the circular drive, it was right behind a red Jaguar. Cliff Drake had gotten there before her, and at an hour early for him. She wondered why he was there. When she went inside, Cliff was nowhere in sight.

Marie was standing in the foyer as if waiting for her.

"Hey," Marie said, sounding tentative, "everything okay this morning?"

Lexie wanted to come back with something about Simon's ghost avoiding her, but considering what she'd seen—or thought she'd seen—on the way home, she couldn't make jokes about it.

"I'm good. Tired, but good."

"You're not still angry with me, are you?"

"I wasn't angry with you, Marie. I just spooked myself is all, and I needed to walk it off."

"Oh."

Marie smiled and seemed to relax and Lexie gave her a great big hug. She knew her friend only wanted what was best for her.

Though Lexie was tempted to talk to Marie about what she thought she'd seen the night before, she simply couldn't. Marie would make a big deal over it, say it was a sign, and would pressure her about her personal life more than ever. Better to let Marie feel a little guilty and drop the issue.

"Cliff came by to make a donation to the silent auction," Marie said.

"So that's why he's here. I saw his Jag out front."

"You'll never believe what he's contributing. Think big," Marie said. "Too big to bring into the ballroom. We'll have to use a photo."

"One of his sports cars?"

"Try one of his speedboats."

"You're kidding." Not that Cliff actually needed more than the three he had. "Huh, wish *I* could afford to bid on it." Lexie was sure that, when new, the speedboat had cost him at least six figures. "Where is Cliff, anyway?"

"He and Doug Heller are with Brandon in his office discussing company business."

Looking out from the ballroom across the foyer where Brandon's office sat facing the drive, Lexie grimaced. "What, no shouting? No loud noises? No gunshots?"

Marie laughed. "Not so far."

Though Lexie was joking, she knew full well that Brandon and his Uncle Cliff didn't get along. Brandon had no respect for his fun-loving, hard-living playboy uncle.

The younger Drake brother by more than a decade, Cliff had always been in competition with Brandon's father, Jonathan. In addition to Drake House, Brandon had inherited his father's half of Drake Enterprises, which he'd had no desire to run. Now the steady, levelheaded one in the family, he contented himself with continuing to run the foundation and keeping an eye on his uncle.

Even though Cliff had taken over the CEO position of Drake Enterprises unopposed, he'd kept up the feud, doing his best to outdo, outshine and outfox Brandon. That led to some pretty intense meetings between the two Drake men.

The company was doing well enough, so Cliff must be doing something right, even if he was relying on his business manager, Doug Heller. At least Marie had *told* her Cliff relied heavily on Heller to make many of the decisions concerning the Eastern Shore properties.

Hearing a truck pull up outside, Lexie poked her head out the front door. "Ah, here's part of my crew now. Time to get started."

"Me, too," Marie said. "There are a thousand little details to take care of. Talk to you later."

After putting her crew to work decorating the huge staircase, Lexie reached for her cell phone and realized she'd left it in the SUV. Throwing on her jacket, she ran out and fetched it. The air was cold and crisp, the sky gray. Snow was imminent; it would replenish the half-melted piles on the ground, and just in time to accentuate the majesty of Drake House for the coming guests. Hopefully, it wouldn't actually snow on the night of the ball.

Opening the entry door, Lexie stepped inside and saw Cliff with the maid, Isabella Faust, a pretty young thing with huge blue eyes and waves of auburn hair. In her early twenties, Isabella was half Cliff's age, not that he wasn't attractive, his slim, six-foot frame usually hung in Armani or some other designer suit.

Marie had told Lexie that Isabella was Cliff's newest romantic interest, making Lexie wonder why he didn't have more discerning taste in women. Marie had also admitted that Isabella was a gold digger, and that the maid had seemed possessive of Brandon— not that Brandon had fallen for her charms.

"So you'll meet me at the Duck Blind as soon as you get off work?" Cliff asked the young maid.

"I might. Convince me."

Cliff leaned over and whispered something in her ear that made Isabella giggle.

Lexie rolled her eyes. Cliff couldn't resist flirting with an attractive woman. Not that he had ever flirted with her, maybe because she'd had Katie so young. He'd always treated both of them with respect.

"All right, then, it's a date," the maid said, her voice throaty as she sauntered off, rotating her hips for Cliff's maximum enjoyment. Indeed, he stared after her until she was out of sight.

Then Lexie said, "Hey, Cliff."

Cliff turned to face her, his handsome features lighting up and the corners of his green eyes crinkling with pleasure. "Oh, there are you are. I just had a look around. It's going to be the most beautiful setting for the charity ball ever. Such talent."

"You have to say that since I take care of the

landscaping for Drake Enterprises, as well as for your home."

"You're more than a caretaker, Lexie. You're an artist. Never undersell yourself."

Lexie grinned. As far as she was concerned, Cliff wasn't a bad sort, despite his reputation.

"I heard about your very generous donation for the silent auction," she said. "Tired of plying the bay waters around here?"

"Hardly. It's one of my favorite pastimes."

"I thought maybe you were getting a new hobby."

"More like a new speedboat. You know me. XSMG builds the Bugatti Veyron of the sea. It travels over 100 miles per hour. I couldn't resist more speed!" His grin infectious, Cliff then sobered to ask, "So how's your Katie doing?"

"Growing up way too fast. My baby told me she's going to learn to cook."

"Good for her. She seems like a really good kid. One to make you proud."

"So proud it scares me sometimes." Lexie still remembered what growing up had been like. "I sometimes wonder if she has some secret life I don't know about."

Cliff's smile faded. "Secret life?"

"Just a mother's paranoia. You know, when something seems too good to be true, it often is."

Before Cliff could say anything more, the front

door opened and Doug Heller came in. He ran a meaty hand over his close-cropped, sandy-brown hair. "Hey, boss, we gotta get going."

"In a minute, Heller."

Heller's jowly face tightened. "We got that meeting, remember."

Cliff's jaw clenched and unclenched. "All right." Then to Lexie, he said, "I'm just a slave to the job. You say hi to Katie for me, would you? And don't worry about her or any secret life she might be leading. If you think she's a good kid, then she is. Kids pick up on that, meet your expectations."

"Thanks, Cliff."

Lexie stared after him as he left, taken aback by his last statement.

Had he been talking about himself?

Had his father expected him to be the unreliable one and so he'd proven his father correct by becoming the town playboy? Whatever his reason for the advice, Lexie thought it was kind of him to be concerned about any worry she might have over her daughter.

Cliff Drake might be the wild playboy of the Drake family, but he had a good heart. Several years back, Thornton Garden Center had been in trouble. It had looked like they might have to close up shop—or at the very least scale back to a flower and plant shop, which wouldn't have made enough profit to support her and Katie, her parents and her sister, Carole.

Then Cliff personally had sought her out to redesign the landscaping at Drake Enterprises, when in truth, it hadn't needed to be redone. The following season, he'd hired her to redo the Manor at Drake Acres gardens.

Lexie had always wondered if Cliff had hired her because he felt sorry for her. His kindness had given the business a well-needed boost. In the meantime, word spread about her landscaping capabilities, and the next thing Lexie knew, she had enough work to keep the family business afloat.

She would always be grateful to Cliff for that.

Lexie got back to work. Rather than taking lunch, she ate the sandwich she'd brought while giving instructions to workers putting up small tables near the dance floor, set in front of a low stage that would hold the band. Two high school kids who'd begged her for a way to make some Christmas money came in after school and set up a trio of different-size balsam trees at the far end of the ballroom, decorating them with hundreds of tiny white lights.

By the end of the day, she was feeling good about their progress.

Before leaving, she went in search of Marie, who was in the huge kitchen equipped with stainless steel work areas to handle banquets and a more intimate marble counter area for the smaller family and employee meals. That's where she found Marie with Isabella and the housekeeper Shelley Zachary.

In her midfifties, Shelley had an iron strength—both physically and psychologically—despite her slender appearance. Her hair was pulled back from a narrow face and her thin brows were penciled over eyes that always seemed to be inquisitive. Or so Lexie thought, after Marie told her to watch what she said around Shelley, since the housekeeper was a known gossip. Rather than hiring another butler after the murder of Edwin Leonard, Marie's father, Brandon wanted Shelley to run the house, so the woman had moved into Edwin's quarters off the kitchen, making Lexie wonder if Marie's business was going to be all over town if she wasn't careful.

At the moment, Marie, Shelley and Isabella were at the marble counter area polishing the silver flatware that would be used at the ball.

"Wow, I can see I've got the easy job," Lexie said.

Marie grinned. "That's because you're not domesticated. I'd rather do this any day than haul plants and trees around." She held up a serving piece and inspected it. "There's something satisfying about bringing out the beauty in…well, anything silver."

"A woman in love will fool herself into thinking real work is fun," Lexie teased in return. "I just wanted to let you know I'm done for the day and everything is in good shape."

"Wait! Before you go…" Marie reached into her pocket to retrieve something. "I meant to ask you about this key yesterday, but it slipped my mind. It was found on the grounds where you and your crew did some winter prep work last week. I thought it might be yours."

All eyes were on the brass key as Lexie took it from Marie. Unique in design, it was solid and heavy—an old-fashioned, barrel-type key with a fancy leaf at the top.

"I've never seen this before," Lexie said, "but maybe it belongs to one of my crew."

"Keep it and show it to them, then. It doesn't fit any of the doors in this house."

"Will do."

Giving the key a last look, Lexie realized that Isabella and Shelley weren't the only ones interested. Ned Perry, nattily dressed as usual, his brown hair neatly combed to one side, was there, as well. The annoying land developer who was trying to get his hands on any available waterfront property was standing in the doorway, his gaze glued to the key. She quickly pocketed it in her sheepskin jacket.

Ned practically jumped and cleared his throat. He looked past her to the other women. "Is Brandon home?"

"No, he's not, Ned," Marie said. "And he's not interested in selling any shoreline land, either."

"I'm sure if he hears me out, he'll see things differently. New building would revitalize the area."

Lexie waved to Marie and quietly left the room. As she headed down the hallway, she thought about how the cutthroat developer wanted the Drake Enterprises-held shoreline so that he could build luxury condominiums and make himself a fortune.

She was glad that Brandon didn't want to sell. So much new building would change Jenkins Cove, and not necessarily for the better. In summer the roads were already congested with tourist vehicles. A new development of the size that Ned envisioned would mean congested roads all year round. Not to mention the myriad other problems that would result from nearly doubling the population of a small community all at once.

Once outside, she took a deep breath of fresh air and tilted her face up to the sky. Snow was coming down in big, fat, lazy flakes. Smiling, she climbed into her SUV and took off.

Her smile didn't last long because she'd barely gone a mile before a higher area with scrubby brushes and pines came into view to her left. The sun had already set, casting long shadows over the area. She could see one of the pieces of heavy machinery parked there and a Jenkins Cove police vehicle parked off road, the cop inside apparently keeping an eye on the site. The state was still digging up the mass grave found earlier in the month as part of its investigation into human trafficking. They were still finding bodies.

So many deaths in such a small town…Lexie's mind went back to Simon dying so young. Marie really was right. Simon was gone and she had to stop thinking about him. Definitely had to stop dreaming about him, she thought, flushing.

Lexie was glad to reach Thornton Garden Center, a long, low brick building with big windows filled with glass sun catchers and red poinsettias and amaryllis.

Upon entering, Lexie looked for her mother. She gazed around the store, but didn't see her among the customers, who were mostly checking out the Christmas ornaments in baskets set among the plants in the windows. Her sister, Carole, an older, shorter version of Lexie, except for her henna-enhanced, reddish-brown hair, was at the register behind the counter.

"Hey, is Mom out back with Dad?"

Her father was in charge of the landscaping supplies sold in the attached sheltered area, and during the holiday season, the Christmas trees in the outside area beyond.

"Nope. She made him take her home early. She's in her cookie-making mode and couldn't think about anything else. Phil took over for Dad."

"I didn't get my invitation to join you."

Carole just laughed. "Is that why you're gunning for Mom?"

"If I didn't give her a hard time about it, she would think something was wrong."

Though she was exhausted, Lexie went to the far side of the counter and checked her desk/design center and found a message from one of her business customers requesting more poinsettia plants and a couple of wreaths for the company Christmas party next week. No sense in waiting until the morning. She called Phil on the intercom and told him what she needed just as the police chief entered and walked to the other end of the store, straight to the refrigeration unit holding floral arrangements.

A squat bulldog of a man, Chief Hammer was no one's favorite. He had a reputation for letting things slip by him. Lexie had always thought he was just plain lazy. Thankfully, the state had taken over the mass grave tragedy. If it was up to Hammer, he would probably have left the bodies where they were and buried the investigation. Pulling a bouquet from the refrigerator, he made his way to the counter just as Phil Cardon came from the back, carrying a couple of wreaths.

Probably in his early thirties, Phil was a seasonal worker for the garden center. He made his living doing odd jobs in town and looked the part, wearing scruffy jeans, work boots and a raggedy jacket.

"These are what we have left right now. Do you think they're big enough for a business?"

"They're on the small side." Lexie frowned. She didn't want to disappoint a good customer. "When you make the delivery, check with the administrative assistant, Rosemary. Tell her if she can wait until Monday, we can make up a few bigger ones for her."

"Okay." He turned to go.

Remembering that Phil had been part of her grounds crew at Drake House, Lexie said, "Wait a minute." She pulled the key from her jacket pocket. "Someone lost this on Drake property. Any chance it's yours?"

Phil pushed straggly brown hair from his eyes and shook his head. "Not mine."

"If anyone mentions a lost key, let me know."

Phil nodded and headed toward the back.

"Lost key, huh?" Chief Hammer said from the counter, where Carole was wrapping his flowers. "Can I see it?"

Not knowing why, Lexie was reluctant to hand the key over to him. She let it nestle in her palm and kept it out of his reach.

"Unusual key." He held out his hand, indicating she should turn it over to him. "Maybe I should take it for safekeeping until the rightful owner claims it."

"It'll be safe enough with me." Lexie closed her hand. "I'll see my other workers tomorrow. I'm sure one of them dropped it."

"Here you go, Chief," Carole said.

Hammer stared at Lexie for a moment before turning to take his purchase.

What was that all about? she wondered as the police chief left. No doubt one of Hammer's little power plays. He liked being seen as the big man in town even if he didn't want to do the work that came with the designation.

Realizing that she still had the key in her hand, she slipped it into a back pocket where it would stay put.

"You look beat," Carole said. "Maybe you ought to go home and take a bubble bath or something."

"Or something," Lexie agreed, suppressing a yawn. Right now, her bed called to her. "Are you sure you don't need me?"

Carole rolled her eyes. "I lock up in less than half an hour. Just go."

"Okay, then." Lexie slipped into her jacket and headed for the door. "Have a good time tonight. Tell Mom I expect to have enough cookies to gorge on."

Thoroughly exhausted, Lexie was glad the drive home was short. Snow was still falling, but there was little new accumulation. Five minutes later, she pulled up in the gravel parking area next to the house. Yawning while clambering out of the SUV, she dragged herself toward the front door and pulled her keys out of her shoulder bag.

Almost to the door, she heard a shuffle behind her. Heart thumping, she turned to see a figure dressed in dark clothing, face covered by a ski mask, advance on her.

The man she'd seen the night before?

Was he stalking her?

Though her chest squeezed tight, she tried not to panic.

Knowing she couldn't make it inside, Lexie threw her shoulder bag as hard as she could and hit him square in the face, then ran, her pulse jagging. She heard him curse and come after her. Not interested in money, then.

Her heart hammering, she ran flat out around the house, hoping to reach the wood stack in back, where she could arm herself with a split log. Maybe she could knock the man out, *then* get inside.

In the side yard, she slipped on the snowy grass and nearly fell, the interruption long enough for her attacker to catch up to her. Her scream for help was cut off when he tackled her.

She went down hard, her breath knocked out of her, yet struck back with the hand holding her keys. Before she could connect with his head, he grabbed her wrist and pounded it against the ground. The keys went flying into the snow. Undaunted, Lexie continued to fight and squirm away as the man started feeling her up.

Weirdly, the attack didn't seem sexual in nature. It was as if her assailant were searching for something…patting her jacket pockets and trying to get his hands inside them.

Though she bucked and struck out, she was unable to get him off her. "What do you want?"

When he didn't answer, she clawed at the mask.

He knocked her hand away and hit her in the head so hard her vision went out of focus and her limbs went limp so that she had to struggle to remain conscious.

He was slipping his hands under the jacket now, feeling the sides of her jeans. Had she been wrong about this not being sexual? Her stomach lurched and she was about to renew her battle, when suddenly her attacker rose off her as if by magic.

Lexie took a deep breath and scooted back to see her masked assailant struggling with another man. A tall and broad man with spiked, light brown hair and heavy-lidded eyes.

Unless she really was seeing a ghost, it was…

"Simon?"

Chapter Four

Lexie's cry caught Simon off guard and the bastard who'd attacked her got a moment's advantage, nearly delivering a kidney punch. Honed reflexes allowed Simon to drop and divert the blow. He landed on one knee, and when the attacker kicked out, he grabbed the bastard's foot and twisted. The man flipped around and landed on the ground.

Lexie was groaning, and Simon gave her a quick glance to see her struggling to her feet.

Enough time for the attacker to get to his feet and run off.

Though Simon would have liked to go after the bastard, he was more concerned about Lexie.

Fearing that she was hurt, he swept her up into his arms. "Let's get you into the house."

"Keys," she whispered with a groan, indicating the area to the right of where she had fallen.

Simon moved in that direction, carefully sweeping the snowy ground with his gaze. There was just enough light to see the skid marks made by the keys. He reached out blindly and felt around for a few seconds before feeling metal against his fingertips.

"Got 'em."

Lexie seemed to be coming back to herself. She started pushing against him. "Let me down. I can walk."

"I'm sure you can."

Not that Simon was about to let her down. He carried her around the house to the front door, picking up her shoulder bag along the way.

As he sorted through the keys, he felt Lexie's gaze on him, but he didn't look at her. He hadn't meant for this to happen. He'd been unable to keep himself from spying on her.

"I missed you all these years, Simon. You don't know how much. That's why I let Marie talk me into going to the psychomanteum yesterday." Seeming confused, only half-aware, Lexie continued babbling. "I wanted to see you one last time before I said goodbye forever. Now that I have, I don't want to let you go."

Simon realized that the smack from her attacker must have scrambled her brains. He got her inside, kicked the door closed behind them, then carried her to the oversize couch, upholstered in a brown and burgundy design, and gently set her down against the myriad pillows.

"Let me look into your eyes."

"I always loved it when you looked deep into my eyes and I looked into yours…"

She was trying to do that now.

"I want to make sure you don't have a concussion." Kneeling in front of her, he pulled a pencil-thin maglite from the pocket of his leather bomber jacket and, lifting her chin a bit, shone the light in her eyes. "Your pupils are even and dilating properly. No concussion."

So why was she so confused?

Psychomanteum? What the hell was that?

Suddenly Lexie blinked and her expression shifted. As if testing, she poked him in the chest. "Wait a minute, you're no ghost! You're alive!"

Simon got to his feet and backed away. "That I am."

The confusion cleared, leaving shock in its place. "But they told me you were dead!"

"I assure you, I am very much alive, Lexie."

"Oh my God!" Lexie lunged off the couch and threw herself against him. "You're alive! You're really alive!" she said through her tears.

And then she kissed him, plunging him back thirteen years, to the night they'd made love, had made plans to start a life together, away from Jenkins Cove. Instead, he'd started a new life without her. A life he would never be able to forget…or share with her.

He didn't want her to know what he had become.

So it was he who broke the kiss and pushed away the one person in the world who meant anything to him. The only woman he'd ever loved.

"Simon?" Lexie blinked and wiped away her tears, focused on his face as if really seeing him for the first time. "Simon…if you weren't dead…why didn't you come for me? Why did you leave me? I've spent thirteen years mourning you. What happened? You simply chose to play dead and on the very night I was going to run away with you?"

"I had no choice in what happened to me."

Lexie shook her head. "We all have choices."

Her accusing expression and tone put Simon's back up. "Not always. Sometimes things are out of our control."

"For thirteen years? You walk out of my life and don't contact me? Don't let me know what happened or even that you're still alive?"

"I couldn't."

He couldn't at first. But by the time his situation had changed, so had he. He'd become a man Lexie didn't know. Wouldn't want to know. One he hadn't wanted her to know. He'd wanted her to be happy, to have a good life, and it looked like she did…though she wasn't wearing a ring and he didn't see signs of another man.

The room was all Lexie—casual yet with a hint

of sophistication. The couch, a matching chair in front of the fireplace, a leather chair with a scrolled back by the windows, maybe for reading. The lamps had shades of stained glass or mica; the accessories on mission-style tables were feminine in design. Nothing to indicate that a man lived here.

That kiss Lexie had given him had certainly been hungry enough…

Suddenly she said, "Get out!" Her face was flushed, her expression angry.

"What? You were just attacked."

"Thank you for saving me," she said evenly. "I'm fine now, so you can go back to wherever you've been hiding for the last thirteen years. You know where to find the door."

"I'm not going anywhere. Someone has to protect you."

"I've had to do that for myself since you left, and you're not someone I can count on!"

The truth of that struck Simon like a physical blow. Too much time had gone by. He couldn't possibly connect with Lexie the way he had in that other life.

"Let me take you to see a doctor—"

"I'm fine. I don't need a doctor. I don't need *you*. Just go, please."

Simon clenched his jaw so he wouldn't argue with her. She probably *was* fine. He had a lot of experience dealing with injured men on the battle-field, and though she had exhibited some strange behavior, he chalked that up to the shock of seeing a dead man. She'd gotten over that quickly enough. She appeared ready to do battle again.

"At least tell me that you'll file a police report." Simon had every reason for staying dead for the moment, at least until he figured out who had sent him to that hell and why he hadn't simply been killed, as had the kid he'd seen murdered. He had to stay dead until he exacted the revenge he sought, his reason for being. "Just don't mention me."

"As far as I'm concerned," Lexie said caustically, "you're still dead and buried."

THE REAL SHOCK of Simon's being alive didn't hit Lexie until he finally left. Alive. After all these years. It hardly seemed real to her.

And then another thought hit her. Katie. What was she going to do about that? Her chest squeezed tight. If she told Simon he had a daughter, would he want to meet Katie only to abandon her, too? He hadn't said anything about staying and she couldn't bear to see her daughter's heart broken as hers had been. She knew just how awful that felt.

Protecting her daughter from emotional pain was her main responsibility here. Thankfully, Katie was staying with her grandparents for a few days. The pressure on her chest let up a little. She wouldn't have to make the decision as to whether to tell Simon just yet. Perhaps she would never see him again. How would she know?

Lexie called the police and got the runaround about no one being there; the chief would call her back. Fat chance. She waited half an hour, then decided to go in and make the report in person.

Trying to keep her teeming emotions under control, Lexie got her keys and started for the front door.

Afraid that her attacker might still be out there, however, she decided to check and went from window to window to stare out into the dark. Her pulse spiked, but she saw nothing, no one.

Not even Simon.

Heart hammering, Lexie grabbed her bag, slipped out of the house, raced to her SUV, got inside and immediately locked herself in. She drove straight to the police station, an old house a block off Main Street, bought by the city to house offices for its small force.

"Hey, Lexie," Martha, the dispatcher/receptionist at the front desk, said when she entered. "Chief Hammer just got in."

"Good." Without waiting to be announced, Lexie headed for his office. The door was open, so she walked right in. "I want to report an attempted robbery."

Frowning, Hammer looked up from his newspaper. "Something happen after I left the garden center?"

"Not there, at my home. I was attacked."

"What was stolen?"

"Nothing. I, uh, fought him off."

"If nothing was stolen…"

Lexie seethed. He didn't want to write up the report. As usual, Chief Hammer was trying to get out of doing any work.

"What if I was hurt?"

"Are you?"

"Not really." Though the side of her face was still a bit sore where the attacker had hit her.

"You know, Lexie, it was probably some out-of-towner just looking for money during the Christmas season. You should have given up your pocketbook and he would have fled."

Yeah, that would have made things easier for everyone. Lexie clenched and unclenched her jaw. "He didn't want my bag. He had me on the ground and his hands were all over me and—"

Hammer raised his hand for her to stop. "Draper!" he yelled. "I need you to take a report."

The police chief really *was* adept at avoiding work.

A young officer named Sam Draper appeared at the door and waved her out of the room and over to a desk where he took her report. He hemmed and hawed to himself a bit before saying, "If this guy was interested in robbing you, I don't get why he didn't just take your shoulder bag."

"You and me both." She didn't want to say she'd been rescued. She didn't want anyone to know that Simon was alive any more than he did.

"You say he had you on the ground and was feeling your, um, pockets?"

"Right."

"Any idea of what your attacker could have been looking for?"

She shook her head. "No." Not until that moment. Suddenly she thought of the key Marie had given her. The key she'd slipped into her back pocket. She stopped herself from feeling for it to make sure it was still there. She wiggled her butt against the back of the chair and felt something hard that must be the key. Thinking caution would serve her well at this point, she said, "No idea at all."

Draper said, "I really don't know that we'll be able to get this guy, being that he was wearing a mask and all. Are you sure you can't identify something about him? Height? Body type? Something about his hands?"

"Nothing. I'm sorry. I was so freaked…it…it seemed like a nightmare."

"Tell you what I'll do. I'll follow you home and drive around your place, give the area a good look-see to make sure the guy's gone."

Lexie nodded. "Thanks, I'd appreciate it."

"Let's go, then."

Only when she rose and turned to go did Lexie realize that Chief Hammer was leaning against his office doorjamb. He'd been watching her the whole time, but she had no clue what he was thinking. His face was expressionless.

Draper followed her home in the police vehicle, an SUV, then pulled up next to her and rolled down his window. "Stay put while I circle the area, make sure it's safe."

"Will do."

She followed Draper's progress with her gaze until his vehicle disappeared behind a stand of trees. Her thoughts wandered, going from the key and what her attacker might want from it to Simon.

Where had he been all these years? Why had he left in the first place? He'd said he had no choice. How was that possible? Lexie began regretting sending him away without getting answers to her many questions.

Startled from her thoughts as the police vehicle pulled up next to her again, she lowered her window. Moonlight silvered Draper's half-regretful expression.

"No one around," he said. "Wish I coulda got the guy for you, but at least you're safe. House looks locked up tight, too. I can check inside if you want."

"Thanks."

Lexie rolled up her window and grabbed her shoulder bag, then slid out of her SUV. Moving to the entrance, grateful that Draper was watching her back, she unlocked the door, then, pulse quickening, she let him in first and quickly followed. Minutes passed, seeming like forever. He came out of the kitchen, gave her a thumbs-up and headed upstairs. Lexie breathed normally only when he came back down.

"All clear."

"I really appreciate your looking out for me."

He gave her a crooked smile and tipped his hat. "My job."

"Thanks, anyway."

Closing the door after him, Lexie would like to think this was the end of it, that her attacker wouldn't be back, but she wasn't so certain that was true. She went around the house, closing the blinds.

At least Katie was with her parents and sister for a few nights and didn't have to be afraid. Her parents... She would have to call them. Sam Draper's wife was one of the town gossips. Shelley Zachary, Brandon's housekeeper, being the other. Lexie was sure that everyone would know what had happened by morning.

She couldn't let her parents hear it from someone else, so she would have to call them and tell them what happened, leaving Simon out of the story.

Though she hated lying, Lexie couldn't tell anyone Simon was back. Not yet, anyway.

Before making the call, she needed to put the key someplace safe until she could figure out why it was so important. But where? She looked around the room, her eyes lighting on the staircase. There was a hollow in the newel. She and Katie had used it to hide messages to each other ever since Katie learned to write. No one else knew about their special hiding place. Since Katie wasn't going to be home for a couple of days, the key would be safe there.

Taking the key from her back pocket, she unscrewed the newel.

"Why are you so special someone would attack me to get hold of you?" she murmured, turning the key in her fingers.

No answer came to her. How would she ever figure it out?

Setting it in the hiding place, Lexie went to the phone to make that call to her parents.

Chapter Five

Not wanting his presence known until he figured out the mystery of his past and a way to avenge the horror that had been done to him, Simon had camped out where he and Lexie used to go to be alone—a fishing shack in a stand of trees about a hundred yards from the water. To get there, he had to pass the swampy area that everyone in town always avoided—which had just been revealed as a mass grave.

On the way to the shack now, Simon slowed his truck when he neared the Duck Blind, which his father owned, at the west end of town, where the commercial buildings trailed off. Rufus was just coming out of the bar-restaurant. His salt-and-pepper hair had thinned a bit as had his still-muscular body. Even from a distance, Simon could see the short, scraggly beard he'd always had. To Simon's surprise, his father didn't seem to be drunk. His hand was steady as he locked the door and he walked a straight line heading for the only car left in the small lot to one side of the building.

As far as Simon could tell, his old man was stone-cold sober.

Warmth flooded through him, and he realized that his father's apparent sobriety made him happy. There had been times when he'd felt his father really had loved him, though mostly that had been before his mother died and Rufus hadn't been drinking so heavily. Afterward, his father had immersed himself in booze.

Thinking about the old man had always plunged Simon in a dark mood. Now perhaps he would have reason to put those bad memories behind him. He only wished his father could have sobered up when he was still around. If he had, things would have gone very differently in Simon's life.

A thought that made him stay in the truck.

He wanted to catch up with his father, but he wasn't ready to do so just yet. Their rocky relationship was still too clear in his mind, especially the argument that had made Simon decide to run away. He'd tried to talk his father into cutting back on the drinking. He'd even poured half a bottle of whiskey down the drain. The old man had responded with his fists and by saying that Simon was no son of his.

That had broken Simon's heart.

The wound had never healed, and yet Simon

watched from where he'd stopped near the tree line until his father drove off.

Then he went on his way, driving as far as he dared. He'd found a place to hide his truck in a stand of pine trees before reaching the swampy area where, as the media had reported, dozens of bodies had been found, some from deaths a century ago; many others more recent.

Who had done this to them? The same man responsible for his fate? He'd spent years dreaming about using the skills he was learning on the man. In his mind, he'd punished the bastard for what he'd done in every way possible.

But if the same man was responsible for this atrocity…

Tentacles of fog wove throughout the area, but Simon could still see the crime scene tape and several pieces of heavy equipment that had been left alongside the excavation. Usually there was a cop car somewhere around—the reason he didn't want to take his truck all the way to the fishing camp, lest he be spotted. But tonight the police seemed to be elsewhere.

Simon wondered how many more bodies would be found.

The mass grave reminded him of several incidents in the war-torn areas he'd fought in. There had been no time for funerals and neat graves with headstones commemorating the lives of the dead. They'd been piled one on top of the other, taking away the last of their dignity.

But these dead hadn't been part of a war. From what he understood, these poor souls had been tricked into coming to this country, thinking they would get a better life, but had ended up as spare parts for people who could afford to skip the donor lists.

So much evil in this world. Everywhere. But this was unfathomable.

Simon couldn't make his legs carry him past the mass grave, not without stopping and paying the victims his respect. He bowed his head and said a silent prayer for their souls.

And then he said one for his own.

He, too, had done unforgivable things—not out of choice, but out of necessity—and he was ready to do more. Those responsible for the nightmare he'd survived needed to be dealt with, and Simon didn't believe that justice would be done unless he made sure of it himself. And he was determined that justice would be done.

A chill suddenly swept over him, as if he were standing in a pocket of cold air.

When Simon raised his head and opened his eyes, he saw a figure materializing in the fog. In the stand of pine to the east of the mass grave, a man was staring at him. No, not a man. A teenager with a mop of pale hair over hollow eyes and wearing a light leather jacket and ripped jeans.

Simon's pulse jagged and, for a moment, he forgot to breathe.

The figure was so familiar. Simon would swear this was that kid he'd seen shot thirteen years ago!

It couldn't be.

"Hey!" Simon shouted, forgetting he was trying to stay undercover. "Who are you?"

The ghostly figure gestured to Simon as if asking him to follow before moving off in a swirl of fog. Unable to help himself, Simon complied and followed the kid on a path nearly straight back to his truck and realized this wasn't far from where he'd been taken while on his way to get Lexie that night so long ago. Pockets of icy air rippled along his skin. No matter how hard he tried, how fast he ran, Simon couldn't catch up to the wraith.

Simon absolutely believed that the souls of the departed haunted people. He'd lived with one—the man he'd killed in self-defense—for months in Somalia. Only when he had reconciled his own actions had the dead man's spirit crossed over. Over the years he'd been shadowed by other ghosts, but he'd learned to steel himself against them and they'd eventually left him alone.

Left him empty and hard…damaged goods… without a soul of his own.

So why was he being haunted now? He hadn't been responsible for the kid's death.

What did this lost soul want from him?

Once in his truck, he lost the apparition, had to go slow on the road, searching the land from the road to the water as he drove. He spotted the ghostly figure off and on in between the trees all the way to the edge of town, where he ditched the truck behind a warehouse and followed on foot.

The sidewalks were nearly clear of pedestrians, the streets of vehicles. No one seemed to notice the mist-shrouded kid. Down the block, a stray dog was going about his business, but stopped when the kid drew near. It didn't make a sound, but it froze and its ruff went up and then it warily backed off.

Simon's ruff went up, too.

What the hell?

The kid walked along a red brick fence that surrounded the gray stone church at the center of town, Jenkins Cove Chapel. Suddenly, he disappeared through an opening.

Heart pounding, Simon ran faster so as not to lose him.

The fog was lighter here, the chill greater, and once past the fence's wooden gate, which had been left open, Simon realized where he was.

The cemetery.

Why had the kid brought him here?

Following the curving redbrick path lined by boxwood on both sides, Simon kept track of the kid's mop of pale hair, which appeared on the other side of the hedge, then lost him altogether. When he came to the open area dotted with gravestones and markers, Simon only half hoped he would actually find him again. He gazed around, past a couple of large willow oaks and a magnolia tree in the center of the graveyard, then spotted the kid at a far gravesite, touching the stone that identified its occupant.

Again, the kid looked up at him with hollow eyes and gestured that he should come.

Reluctantly, Simon did. Not wanting to cross anyone's grave—he'd had enough of that in his former life—he stayed on the brick path, keeping his gaze locked on the figure still summoning him.

One minute the fog seemed to circle the kid, the next he seemed to fade away into the mists.

"Wait! Don't go!"

But the demand came too late. The kid was already gone. And Simon was moving to the headstone he'd touched, had obviously wanted Simon to see.

A deep, arctic cold suddenly surrounded Simon and then the breath was knocked out of him as he stopped in the spot where the kid had disappeared. Looking down, Simon understood why Lexie believed he was dead and buried. The headstone bore his name and the dates of his birth and of his supposed death on Christmas Eve thirteen years before.

Not a man who easily believed in what he couldn't see, Simon had no doubts about who had led him here. Of who was buried in his grave. He was certain the kid he'd seen shot had taken his place.

Thirteen years ago and his ghost still wandered, unable to rest, Simon thought.

How many ghosts inhabited this area?

How many souls were denied eternal rest?

He reached out to touch the headstone as if he could communicate more easily with the dead. The stone was icy, but if he'd really thought he could bring back the kid's ghost or otherwise resurrect him, he would have been sorely disappointed. Nothing happened. No surprise.

Of one thing he was certain. The kid had been buried in his stead. How had they pulled that one off? He and the kid looked nothing alike. A closed coffin, then? How had he supposedly died so that no one would have raised the alarm? Who had been in on his supposed death?

More questions that needed answering.

Another reason for him to stay undercover awhile—to find the answers.

Did *ghosts* seek retribution? he wondered.

Considering the evil that had stalked the town unchecked, probably not.

But now the town had to deal with *him.*

Heart heavy, Simon headed for his truck and a short while later drove past the mass grave. Still no cop, so he drove all the way to the fishing shack and did the best he could to hide the vehicle on the camp's far side.

Had he really returned to Jenkins Cove to seek revenge for what had happened to him? Simon did want to identify the one responsible and learn the reason behind it, did want that person brought to justice, but somehow he wasn't as energized by the thought as he had been when the news about the mass grave had hit the media.

Then he'd convinced himself that's why he needed to come back—to expose everything associated with his own abduction—but the doctor responsible for harvesting organs was dead and his business ended, so what could he really accomplish? No doubt many secrets had died with the doctor, including ones that had to do with him.

Drake Enterprises had been implicated in the modern-day slave trade, but the authorities had barely begun their investigation. According to a newspaper article, the Drake connection didn't seem to hold water. There simply was no evidence, just the word of a man who was not only dead, but who had been crazed with grief at the loss of his wife, another victim.

Simon still wanted answers, certainly, and he wasn't above exacting retribution, as well.

But more than either, he wanted Lexie Thornton. After seeing her, Simon faced the truth: He'd been lying to himself all along.

Even though he knew she wouldn't want him once she learned the truth about how he'd spent the last thirteen years, Simon admitted he'd come back to Jenkins Cove so that he could reclaim the woman he loved.

As he approached the shack, a crack like a twig breaking underfoot froze Simon to the spot. Someone was there, on the other side of the camp. The cop who should have been at the mass grave?

Silently backing up, Simon was about to step behind a tree when he spotted the silhouette of the intruder.

A silhouette he would know anywhere.

What the hell was Lexie doing out here?

AGITATED BY THE ATTEMPTED robbery and even more so by knowing that Simon wasn't really dead, Lexie hadn't been able to settle down for the night. She might not be able to do anything about the assault, but she sure as hell could do something about Simon. She could get the truth out of him. Then just maybe she would tell him about his daughter. Above all, she had to think of Katie. She no longer even knew this man who was her daughter's father, but she had to give him a chance to explain himself.

With that in mind, she'd left the house yet again and had driven to the spot where Katie had been conceived. Somehow she'd known Simon would be here. The moment she saw him, her pulse picked up and her breath shortened.

"What are you doing, Lexie, wandering around in the dark and after being attacked?"

Not exactly the welcome she'd hoped for, but then why should she have expected him to be any friendlier than she had been when she'd thrown him out. Her eyes were adjusting to the dark and there was just enough moonlight to see his mouth set in a straight line.

"We have some things to settle," she said.

"Such as?"

"The last thirteen years."

"I'd rather forget them."

"I can't forget, Simon. What happened? Why did you leave without me?" She'd been going over and over the possibilities and only one thing had occurred to her. "The kid who was buried in your grave… Was there some kind of…accident?"

"Don't you mean, was I responsible for his death?"

Lexie shuddered. She really didn't want to know the answer if it was yes, but she couldn't keep herself from asking, "Were you?"

"No."

His answer was flat, emotionless, like his expression. Lexie believed him. She sensed that he was closing himself off from her. Once that happened, he would never tell her anything, so she moved closer and tried to connect with him by placing a hand on his chest. His heart immediately sped up and she felt him soften toward her, despite the determination she remembered so well.

"Please, Simon, I need to know the truth." Touching him made her a little breathless. She stepped in even closer, looked up into his face, now only inches from hers. "When they told me you were dead, I wanted to die, too."

Simon grabbed her by both arms. "Lexie, don't ever say that. You don't know anything about death."

She could feel every one of his fingers leaving a print on her flesh. Energized from the contact, from the wanting he stirred in her, she asked, "And you do?"

"Too much."

"Now you have to tell me or my imagination will just make things up."

"Reality can be worse than anything you could imagine, believe me."

"My God, Simon," she whispered, moving into him and laying her head on his chest as she used to. Tears filled her eyes as she asked, "What terrible things happened to you that you can't even talk about them?"

But suddenly knowing didn't seem as important as her being close to him. He wrapped his arms around her, pressed her to him so that she could hardly breathe. Her heart fluttered and a gasp escaped her.

How could she be so susceptible to him after so long? She felt exactly as she had thirteen years ago. Exactly as she had dreamed of ever since. She'd ached for this feeling that she'd had with Simon alone. She couldn't let it go. No other man had so stirred her emotions. Or her passion.

So when he kissed her, she couldn't resist.

And when he picked her up and carried her into the old shack that was barely more than half-rotting boards with a single window, she didn't protest.

And when he placed her on the sleeping bag near the cast-iron stove and covered her with his body, she didn't stop him.

Simon was a bigger man, weighed more than he had the last time—the only time they'd made love, but Lexie reveled in the difference, felt as if she couldn't get enough of him pressing against her, kissing her.

His kiss went so deep, she swore it touched her soul. She could drown in it. In him.

Closing her eyes, she let herself float, let herself

dream. When he touched her through her clothing, she couldn't stand it, wanted to feel his flesh against hers, and so she pushed him back and sat up so she could pull off her coat and sweater. He did the same, and by the time the sweater was off her head, she saw him stripping down, the moonlight from the single window making his flesh look like silver-blue marble.

Even in the moonlight she could see that the marble was not without flaws. For a moment, she froze, staring at the network of scars that started on the right side of his chest, slithered partway down his abdomen, and picked up halfway down his thigh.

She gaped at the souvenirs of whatever nightmare he had endured, then vowed to help make him forget it when he was with her.

Her fingers fumbled with the hooks of her bra and the next thing she knew he was kneeling and pulling off her boots, then her jeans. She was nude but for the damn bra, and he leaned forward and swept that off as easily as he had everything else.

"I've waited for you for so long," she whispered, running her hands on either side of his head. The crisp cut of his short hair prickled her palms and the sensation spread down her arms to her breasts.

He groaned and ground his mouth against hers as he swept his hand down her middle to her center, already wet with wanting him. He stroked her lightly, each time his fingers entering her more deeply, each time her legs spreading wider until she was fully open and arching up into him.

He found her as easily as if she was home to him. Their union felt like home to her, as well. She closed her eyes and arched harder so that he could go deeper. Her fingers clawed his back as though she could bring him closer, somehow make him part of her, somehow make it impossible for him ever to leave her again. Too quickly he propelled her to another place where the dark sky inside her mind lit with pinwheels of light.

Only when her cry softened to a sob of contentment did he let himself finish, riding her hard and deep, coming only after she dug her fingers into his buttocks and cried, "Now, Simon, now!"

Then he collapsed on her and she took his weight with gratitude. She felt as if all was right in her world, and hoped that this time, it would last forever.

Lexie had always known she would love Simon forever, and now she was convinced of it.

As DAWN STREAKED through the cabin window after a night of continued abandon and little sleep, Lexie allowed her doubts to creep in.

Still snug in the sleeping bag with Simon wrapped around her, as if he never meant to let her go, she looked around the shack and noted what appeared to be the same rickety wooden table and two chairs, the cot with the same thin mattress they'd used last time. Nothing had changed.

No, everything had changed.

Simon's eyes were open, glued to her face. She pushed him until he let go of her, then found her clothes. Luckily sometime during the night, Simon had stacked the stove with wood and there remained embers to keep her warm as she dressed. Simon watched her every move without rising, without saying a word. His expression had closed again, as if he thought she were going to give him her back and walk out on him.

Not likely. Not until she had what she'd come for. The truth.

Suddenly Simon rose and got something out of his supply bag. Coffee. Nude, he set about making a pot on the wood-burning stove. Lexie's breath caught in her throat as sunlight revealed the full beauty of his body. His muscles looked as if they'd been sculpted, his abdomen was flat, his waist trim, his shoulders massive. And his butt—her favorite part of him—was rock hard. Blushing when he turned her way and she noted that wasn't the only part of him that was hard, she amended his butt to her second favorite body part.

"Are you going to have some coffee before you go?" he asked as if she were someone who'd simply stopped by rather than the woman he'd made love to half the night.

"I was hoping for more."

"Let's see, I have beef jerky. And—"

"Not food. The truth, Simon," she said, pulling on her socks. "I was hoping for that."

His expression tightened. "You don't really want to hear it."

Or he really didn't want to tell her. "Let me decide for myself. How, for example, did you get those scars?"

Rather than answering immediately, he reached down, picked up his jeans and stepped into them. Finally, he said, "Human trafficking."

The breath caught in her throat. "Someone removed your organs?"

"Worse. They removed my soul." He didn't sit; rather, he paced, barefooted, the short length of the cabin. "I saw one of the victims killed that Christmas Eve. He was just a kid, younger than I was. He's the one buried in my grave. He was trying to escape and they shot him dead. I should have run. Maybe they would have shot me, too. That would have been better than what they did to me."

"What who did to you?"

"I don't know. I was knocked out, drugged, and when I came to, I was on a transport ship bound for Africa with a bunch of mercenaries working for a private army employed by the U.S. government." He grabbed his sweater and pulled it on. "They had a contract saying I'd agreed to go with them, to work for them for the next five years. Only it wasn't me who signed the papers."

"Work? You mean…fight?"

"If I hadn't, I really would have died. Maybe I should have."

"Don't say that!"

Her heart thumped against her ribs and Lexie knew that she really didn't want to hear…and that she had to.

"I had to do things that changed me, Lexie. Things you would never understand. I had no choice. I did as I was told and learned to use weapons and my own cunning to stay alive. It was a nightmare of a life—kill or be killed. I couldn't escape. I had no way to get out, no money. My salary was put into a bank account I couldn't access until my tour of duty was over."

"Five years, not thirteen."

How could he have stayed longer? How could he have chosen that life over one that he could have had with her?

"After my contract was fulfilled, I knew I could never come back here and face you. How could I after the life I'd been forced into? So I reupped. Believe it or not, Shadow Ops was a legitimate private military corporation, hired by the Department of Defense to do work for the CIA. They sent us to Somalia, Afghanistan and Iraq."

"We could have been together for years, but you chose to stay in something you hated?"

"I'm a different person than the one you knew."

"But you still have a soul or you wouldn't have worried about who you might hurt coming back here." Tension and doubt filled Lexie with confusion. She felt the same radiate from him. "We could have been together years ago, Simon. But you abandoned us."

"Us?"

Realizing her slip, Lexie said, "Me…your dad…"

"Why would you include him when you know how I felt about him?"

"But after you died…after we *thought* you died, he cleaned up his act."

Simon's gaze seared her. He didn't believe her.

Lexie knew she could go on lying, but he would no doubt eventually learn the truth. Torn between wanting to protect Katie and wanting to tell Simon they'd had a daughter together, she chose the latter and prayed it really was the right thing.

"About six weeks after we buried you, I learned I was pregnant. We have a twelve-year-old daughter, Simon. Her name is Katie."

His shocked expression would be comical if it weren't so tragic. Lexie's chest tightened as she waited for his response. One that didn't come. Why didn't he say something? Didn't he care that they had a daughter?

Suddenly furious, meaning to get out now, she pulled on her shoes and grabbed her coat. Simon took hold of her arm and stopped her from heading toward the door.

"Tell me."

"She's a good kid. Smart. Smart mouth, too, sometimes. Old for her age. She's had to be with only one parent who has to make a living to support her and take care of her. She looks pretty much like I did at that age, except for her eyes. Those are yours."

She gave him time to process the information. Minutes ticked by and he didn't respond. Didn't say how happy he was to learn he had a kid.

Maybe he wasn't.

Lexie pulled free, cursing herself for falling into Simon's arms so easily when obviously the last thirteen years had left him devoid of normal human feelings.

Chapter Six

Simon moved fast, blocking Lexie's access to the door. "I thought you wanted to talk."

Now all she wanted to do was get away from him before she dissolved into tears. "I'm talked out."

"Maybe I'm not."

"Maybe you're too late, Simon."

She should have known better than to think he cared about a kid he'd never seen, never even knew he'd fathered. She should have known better than to think he cared about her. After all, he'd made no declarations of love during the night.

It had been a mistake to tell him about Katie.

"We'll talk later, then, I promise," he said. "At least let me take you home."

"I have my own vehicle."

"I'll follow you, check the house before you go in."

"Why?"

"To make sure you're safe."

"And how long can I count on your doing that?"

she asked, unable to keep the sarcasm from her voice. "For a few weeks? Days? Just this morning and then you disappear again for another thirteen years? Let me out. Now."

His expression tightening, Simon moved away from the door and Lexie left without looking back.

What a fool she'd been to sleep with him! Driven by hormones and nostalgia, she'd just made the biggest mistake of her life. How had she imagined that Simon Shea was the same person he had been thirteen years ago?

Lexie fumed about her stupidity all the way home. Only when she parked the SUV did her tension switch gears. The fog had lifted and the sun shone brightly. Nothing to alert her. Nothing to fear.

Even so, she held her breath and moved fast and was inside her house in a minute flat.

Only when she let go of her breath and turned from the front door did her heart begin to pound. Even with nothing but faint dawn light edging through the windows, she could see that the place was a mess. Cushions had been pulled from the couch, drawers from her desk. Papers were scattered everywhere. She was about to call the police, when a scraping sound coming from somewhere nearby stopped her.

Whoever it was hadn't left!

She turned to get out of the house, but the lock confounded her shaking hand, and by the time she got the door open a crack, she was grabbed from behind. She kicked back and used her elbows to help twist her way out of his grip and ran toward the rear door. No sooner did she reach the kitchen than her attacker caught up to her and tripped her. She went down hard and he was on her, searching her again.

Lexie fought, beating at him with both fists, trying to knee him, but missing. And this time there was no Simon to pull the bastard off her.

Then he got hold of both her hands.

"What do you want?"

"The key," he demanded. "Hand it over and you'll never be bothered again."

His voice was low and husky coming from behind the knit mask that hid his face.

So she'd been right about the key. What could be so important about it that someone would attack her twice to get it?

"What key?"

"Don't play dumb. You know I mean the one found on the grounds of Drake House."

"Oh, that one." She thought quickly. "I threw that key away."

Gripping both of her wrists together with one hand, he reached in his jacket pocket for something. Her eyes were adjusting to the dim early-morning light and she saw him pull out a roll of duct tape. The next thing she knew, he was taping her wrists together.

"Where is the damn key?" he demanded.

"I told you it's gone."

"Don't lie to me."

"What does it open?" Lexie asked, hoping he would say something that would give her a clue. "A safe-deposit box filled with money or bonds or jewels? Is that why you're so set on getting it?"

"Stop playing games. If you don't want to get hurt, tell me what I want to know."

Remembering that her attacker had hit her before, Lexie went stiff. Still, if the key was important enough to commit a crime to get, she couldn't just turn it over to this bastard.

"I asked around. No one claimed it, so I threw it away," she lied, hoping she sounded convincing.

"Where?"

"In town. The trash can between the police station and the library."

Now he was securing her ankles together with the tape. "I don't believe you."

"Why would I want to keep a key I couldn't use?" Lexie tried not to panic, but keeping an even head wasn't doing her any good. "I swear I don't have it anymore. Why is an old key so important?"

He placed a piece of the duct tape over her mouth. "Maybe I'll have to wait until your girl comes home and ask *her* about it."

Katie? He was threatening Katie now? Behind the duct tape, Lexie screamed.

Too bad no one could hear her.

SIMON WAS DEVASTATED. He'd missed the last dozen years with a kid who was his and Lexie's—years that he wouldn't ever want his child to know about. Perhaps, he thought, it would be better if Katie never knew about him, either.

Saddened by the thought, he sat in his truck down the road from Lexie's house, waiting for lights to go on somewhere. Despite her harsh words, he'd finished dressing quickly and had driven like a maniac until he'd gotten her SUV in sight. Well trained in the art of subterfuge, he'd followed at a discreet distance, and when she'd hit the gravel road, he turned off his truck's lights so that she wouldn't know anyone was behind her.

Still no light in the house.

Getting a bad feeling, Simon left his truck and walked in closer to the house, his gaze shooting from corner to corner. He couldn't see anything wrong, but his gut told him otherwise. When he got close to the front door, he saw that it was open, if just a crack.

His gut tightened.

Lexie would never leave her front door open, not after the attack the night before. He should have forced her to let him go with her, rather than staying in the background as he had.

Listening intently, Simon thought he heard a sound like a muffled voice from another part of the house. Removing a knife from his jacket—carrying a weapon on him for thirteen years was a hard habit to break—he slowly edged the door open until he could see inside. The living room was a mess, but it was empty so he edged himself in and followed the low murmur of a male voice.

"Your girl will tell me what I want to know."

The answer was a muffled protest.

He was talking about Katie, Simon realized, silently moving forward until he saw a dark-clad figure standing over Lexie on the kitchen floor.

The bastard must have sensed him, because he threw a glance over his shoulder, then ran for the back door.

Simon stopped only long enough to cut the tape holding Lexie's hands and feet together, and pulled another strip from her mouth. Then he ran, too.

The assailant had already disappeared. Simon looked down at what was left of the snow on the ground. Tracks led back and forth to one side of the house. By the time he rounded the corner, however, he heard an engine start up. The bastard had parked his vehicle somewhere beyond the stand of trees, just far enough so that Simon couldn't see it until the lights went on. Too late.

He ran anyway, hoping at least to identify the vehicle, but all he got was a glimpse of something dark in the distance. He couldn't even distinguish whether it was a car or a truck or an SUV. Finding where it had been parked, he checked the tire tracks— and he suspected they were made by all-terrain tires with a lot of traction. He took a mental snapshot of the pattern, then shot back to the house.

Lexie wasn't in the kitchen. Hopefully, she was calling the police.

"Lexie?"

"In here."

He followed her voice. Rather than on the phone, he found her at the stairs that led to the second floor. She stood at the newel post, the carved finial in her hand.

"What are you doing?" he asked.

She reached into the shallow depression at the top of the newel post and pulled out something small. "A key. I just wanted to make sure this was still here. This is what he wanted. He said so."

"Then why didn't you give it over? It's not worth your life!"

"I don't know. Instinct. I get the feeling this key unlocks a mystery, as well as a lock."

"Did you call the police?"

She shook her head. "What if the chief's involved? Not that he attacked me himself. But what if he's the one who told the attacker I have the key? When I showed it to Phil—one of my workers at the garden center— Hammer was there. He seemed awfully interested in the key, wanted me to hand it over. I didn't."

"Even when I was a kid, I heard rumors that Hammer could be bought." He moved closer then, and his eyes lit on the vintage key in her hand. It was a barrel key with a decorative leaf at the end. He'd seen one like that before…. Then suddenly, the memory crystalized. "One of the men responsible for my disappearance had a key like that. I was drugged, but I remember seeing it before he slipped it into his pants pocket."

"Did you see his face?"

Simon shook his head. "I only came to for a few seconds and then was out until I awoke on the transport."

"You know what that means—the key must belong to someone involved in the human trafficking business here. Dr. Janecek was undoubtedly already dead when that key ended up on the Drake property. And his assistant, Franz Kreeger, had already committed suicide in his jail cell."

"I read that the authorities think there's something fishy about Kreeger's death, but they haven't been able to prove it," he said.

"Plus they're certain others must have been involved in transporting the people from Eastern Europe to this area to do the harvesting," Lexie said. "This key proves it. Even if the ring isn't operating now, someone involved is still out there, and for some reason this key is too important to him to let go."

Made sense, Simon thought. "If the state investigation turned up anything, it hasn't hit the media."

Lexie shivered visibly. "No, it hasn't. But this might be the clue they're looking for."

"Or at least the one *I'm* looking for," Simon said. "Maybe you'd better give it to me."

Lexie locked gazes with him. "You're not the only one affected by this."

"But I may be the only one who can solve it."

"Pitting yourself against professional investigators? Isn't that taking a bit too much credit?"

"I didn't just learn to kill while I was gone."

Lexie flinched at that. "I'm the one who has access to various places at this time of year—"

"You're not going to try to investigate yourself," he said.

"Why not? I have as much at stake as you do. You might have been shipped off by the owner of this key, but I was attacked for it, my house searched."

With that, Lexie returned the key to its hiding place in the top of the newel post and reattached the finial. Remembering how stubborn she could be, Simon didn't think he could change her mind.

But he could keep her—and their daughter—safe.

"Then we'll work together." He could move in, shadow her if necessary. "I'll bring my things here and—"

"I don't think so."

"You need protection. And don't tell me again how you can protect yourself, not after what just happened."

Lexie needed more than *his* protection unless he could be with her 24/7 until this case was solved, and he had the feeling that wasn't going to happen. It was time to call in reinforcements—professional bodyguards, ones who would have to keep their distance, since he was certain Lexie would never agree to that, either.

Bray Sloane, an old buddy of Simon's from his tour in Afghanistan, ran Five Star Security in Baltimore and had contracts all over the Eastern Shore. Simon had already contacted him; he had Bray's word that he would send help on the spot if Simon needed it.

Well, Simon needed it now to keep Lexie and their daughter safe.

In addition, Bray's wife, Claire, was making it her mission to see if she could find any of the survivors. With her computer skills, she was bound to find any leads available online and would follow them up.

In addition to which, Simon had her place ads for survivors in all the newspapers within a hundred-mile radius of Jenkins Cove. Simon was offering a very generous reward for anyone who would step forward and give him information. Then again, victims who'd been tricked once might not trust anyone to do right by them a second time.

THOUGH LEXIE CONTINUED to resist Simon's attempt to move in with her, deep inside she was tempted to let him. It wasn't the promise of protection, but the feelings for him that she couldn't resist. Obviously, he still had feelings for her, as well, or he wouldn't be so insistent.

Suddenly she remembered her attacker's threat. "I don't want Katie involved in any of this."

"Of course not," he said.

"He said he was going to wait for her to get home and get the information from her." Lexie's pulse picked up at the thought that he could get to her daughter. "Katie doesn't know anything, Simon. And for the moment she's at her grandparents', but what if—"

"She'll be fine." Simon pulled out his cell phone. "Within the hour, I'll have someone watching your parents' house and following Katie wherever she goes."

Lexie wanted to object, but this was her daughter

they were talking about. She couldn't jeopardize her child's safety because of her own stubbornness.

"All right," she agreed. "In the meantime, I'll call Mom and make sure they're not going anywhere this morning. I won't tell her about any of this, though. I don't want her worrying."

"Sensible."

Simon moved into the next room to make his call and, heart fluttering, Lexie dialed her parents' number. It was just about eight. Early, but not so early as to be suspicious.

Her mother answered on the third ring. "Hey, Mom, how are things going over there?"

"Fine, Lexie."

Lexie could hear the questioning note in her mother's voice. "Don't worry, Mom, I'm not going to crash your cookie-making party. I only wanted to know what was going on. Have you already started this morning?"

Sounding relieved, her mother said, "We just finished breakfast. As soon as I get off the phone, we're going to make those Christmas bells Katie loves so much."

Lexie was relieved, as well. "Great, Mom. Is she there?"

"Of course she's here. Do you want to speak to her?" Without waiting for an answer, she called, "Katie…your mother wants to talk to you."

She could hear Katie's irritable voice from a distance. "Tell her she's ruining my life, Nana. And that I'm not planning on trying to talk you into letting me go to that party, so she can relax already and just leave me alone."

Lexie actually smiled. "Let it go, Mom. She's still angry with me."

"Like daughter, like mother."

Lexie had to laugh. "Okay, okay, you can stop rubbing it in now. I love you, Mom. Tell Katie I love her, too."

She was hanging up the phone when Simon returned, carrying a framed photograph of her and Katie taken the summer before at the Fourth of July picnic her family always had. Katie still had long hair in a ponytail and her body hadn't started filling out yet, but she didn't look much different now. Their arms were around each other and they held one big piece of watermelon between them.

"She's beautiful," Simon said, his voice even, as though he were controlling it. "Just like you."

"We made a great kid, Simon."

But the idea of introducing them still didn't sit well with her. He hadn't come back for them…for her. He'd come back to settle his own score and they just happened to be there.

Simon set the photo down on the counter. "So you talked to your mom. Is Katie okay?"

"As well as a preteen can be."

Though his expression was puzzled, he didn't ask her to explain. "The cavalry is on the way."

Lexie got a bowl from the cabinet and started to crack eggs for an omelet. "Good. Now, about the key…"

"We need to figure out what it opens."

To Lexie's surprise, Simon pulled a frying pan from the rack and, opening the package of bacon, started laying down strips in the pan.

"It's so unusual," she said, adding three more eggs to the bowl, "it must belong to an old cabinet or file drawer, something likely owned by one of the Drakes. Drake Enterprises was implicated in the human trafficking ring. The fiancé of one of the victims said they were brought over on a Drake cargo ship. He was crazy with grief over her death, though, and now he's dead, too."

"Hard to say if he actually knew anything or was just making wild accusations."

"Right. So far, the authorities haven't been able to come up with any kind of connection."

"Let's assume Drake Enterprises *is* somehow responsible," Simon speculated. "That would mean either Brandon or Cliff is involved, right?"

"Not Brandon," Lexie said. Surely Marie's fiancé would have nothing to do with anything illegal.

She popped bread in the toaster and started cooking the eggs.

She said, "I don't see it being Cliff, either. He's not the type to get involved in anything serious. He's into yachts and partying and women who are too young for him."

"Then who is the type?"

Lexie thought about it for a moment. "Maybe Doug Heller. I don't know." When it came right down to it, she hated to implicate anyone.

"Heller… Who's he?"

"Cliff's manager. Basically, he's in charge of the Drake properties on the Eastern Shore."

"Right, I think I remember him."

Heller was pretty much a loner, so Lexie didn't know him well, but she didn't want to point fingers. "I don't think he has anything to do with the shipping arm of the company, though."

"Well, someone has to be guilty," Simon insisted. "Someone responsible for bringing the victims here, where their organs were harvested. And if that was done with Drake ships, who else could it be?"

"I hate this," Lexie said, not wanting either Brandon or Cliff to be guilty. Heller was the wild card, as far as she was concerned. "But I hate what happened to a bunch of innocent people even more."

"Not as much as I do," Simon said, his voice

grim. "This is going to sound…well, crazy, I guess…but I saw one of the victims last night."

"What are you talking about?"

"The kid who was shot in the woods. He led me to the cemetery. To the gravestone with my name on it."

"You mean a ghost?"

Simon nodded.

Lexie shivered. "I don't think you're crazy. I have a hard time believing in ghosts myself, but other people around here have claimed to see them lately, too. Maybe it's because they want the people who did this to them brought to justice."

"That's what I want, what I intend to make happen," Simon said, something in his tone sending a spear of ice through her. "Seeing the kid made me wonder how three grown men would react if *they* were visited by a ghost from their past."

"You mean you. But whoever put you on that transport knows you aren't dead."

"But I wonder how they would react if they saw me."

As they ate, Lexie wondered what would happen if they solved this mystery and Simon settled the score. Would he want to stay in Jenkins Cove with her and Katie?

Her heart ticked a little faster as she considered that possibility.

But no matter what she might want for herself,

she had Katie to think of. She couldn't allow her daughter to be hurt. Not physically. Not emotionally. If Katie met Simon, she would probably fall for her dad as much as Lexie had. Before she introduced father and daughter, Simon would have to prove himself, convince her that he could be trusted and care for Katie as much as she did.

Lexie simply couldn't imagine Simon putting down roots here.

More likely, he'd just leave Jenkins Cove in search of the action he'd gotten so used to. Then what would she tell their daughter?

Chapter Seven

On the way back to his digs at the fishing shack, Simon donned an earpiece and called Bray Sloane on his cell. "Any problems getting your men here?"

"None. The one watching the grandparents' home knows that if your daughter leaves for any reason, he isn't to let her out of his sight."

"I saw your other man when I left Lexie's place. You're sure she won't spot him?"

"He'll be invisible."

"Listen, Bray, I owe you."

Bray laughed. "Don't worry, you'll get my bill." And then his voice sobered. "Afghanistan was hell, but a hell I signed up for. What happened to you and those poor people who came to the United States thinking they were going to get a new, safe life…no one deserves that."

"Yeah." Simon didn't know what else to say.

"I've got to see a potential new client later this morning, so I'll be in Easton, about twenty minutes from Jenkins Cove. If you need me for anything, give me a call and I'll be there as soon as I can."

"I'll keep that in mind. Thanks, Bray."

He ended the conversation just as the narrow asphalt road to the hiding place for his truck came into view. Halfway there, he switched from asphalt to dirt and soon turned into a thick stand of pine trees where he parked and left the truck. He needed to catch a few hours' sleep before putting his plan into action.

His thoughts wandered from ghostly pursuits to Lexie to the daughter he'd never seen. A daughter who looked like the woman he loved. Who had his eyes. A yearning came over him and Simon had to shake it away. He needed to stay focused. Emotions were messy and would make him sloppy. Sloppiness could get someone killed…not necessarily him.

He'd seen enough death to last him a lifetime.

The only deaths he wanted to see were those of the people responsible for ruining his life and the lives of so many others.

As he neared the swampy area, Simon's mind wandered back to the wars he'd fought, and he didn't at first hear the voices until he was almost exposed.

"You're sure you don't own this land?"

"Perry, you're becoming a nuisance."

Simon stopped himself from stepping into the clearing. He stayed within the protection of the pines and the shadows they provided. This Perry

guy was of medium height with brown hair combed
to the side—no one familiar to Simon. But the other
guy—dark-haired, tall and thin—seemed familiar,
though his face was scarred and he was leaning
heavily on a cane as he walked toward the two
vehicles parked nearby.

"If you tell me who owns this land, I'll stop
bugging you about your waterfront property."

"You can't build here anyway. It's a graveyard, for
Pete's sake."

Simon realized that, again, there was no cop on
site. Considering that the holidays were upon them,
the police were probably shorthanded.

"They'll get all the bodies out," the guy named
Perry was saying. "No one else will have the guts
to buy it. I can get it cheap, and once I get a development going, no one will even remember what
went on here."

"I've told you before that your schemes don't
interest me. Now I'm even more certain."

"Look, Drake, if you don't cooperate one way or
the other, I can ruin things for you."

Drake? Simon started. This was Brandon Drake.
Scarred and on a cane!

What the hell had happened to him?

Simon had known Brandon since he was a kid.
Four years older than Simon, Brandon had been
one of the high school leaders for summer programs

meant to keep the Jenkins Cove kids out of trouble. Simon remembered him being a little too overbearing. Or maybe he'd just seemed that way to a kid who resented anyone telling him what to do and who already had a chip on his shoulder because of his crappy home life.

"What? Now you're trying to blackmail me?" Brandon's outraged question was barely discernable as they neared the vehicles.

"I need this deal! You sell me that shoreline property I want and I won't talk."

Simon couldn't hear Brandon's response. He stayed hidden until the men drove off.

He stepped away from the trees and considered what he'd heard. This Perry guy seemed way too desperate to buy land; he didn't even care if it was a mass grave. What was up with that? And Brandon Drake most certainly was hiding something. What could Perry know about Brandon that he could use as blackmail?

And did it have something to do with Drake Enterprises being involved in human trafficking?

WHEN SHE APPROACHED the gated entrance that led up to Drake House later that morning, Lexie was wondering about the nondescript silver sedan that seemed to have been following her for several miles. She turned through the opening between the pillars and onto the drive, and glanced up into her rearview mirror. When the other car kept going without slowing, Lexie took a relieved breath and relaxed.

For a few moments, she'd thought her assailant was back for attack number three. This time, Simon was nowhere nearby to save her butt.

The thought jogged her into thinking about Simon, seeing his face in her mind, remembering how good it felt to be in his arms even on a hard floor in front of a woodstove. It also made her wonder what she should do about Simon in relation to their daughter. Should she let Katie know her father was alive?

It was a decision that could wait until later.

Her crew arrived right behind her. Lexie got them organized, hauling in the truckload of mums, gerbera daisies and more greenery right away. She glanced up at the burned part of the mansion, the reason for the flowers. She might be able to hide the remaining scent of burned wood, but she wouldn't be able to hide the visual evidence. Thankfully, guests wouldn't be arriving for the ball until after dark.

All the basics had to be in place before they left today, Lexie thought, on her way to the entry. The next day would be spent decorating the second-floor parlors and the outside entry to the house. Then there shouldn't be much more to do on the day of the ball than to haul in fresh flowers and cover the tables with linens and candles. Not that there wouldn't be a few last-minute details that needed to be taken care of, but that was always to be expected.

Lexie was just about to the front door when her cell rang. Checking the ID and seeing that it was Simon, she decided to stay outside a few minutes longer to take the call so that she could have some privacy. Circling along the drive toward the bay, she flipped the cell open.

A little thrill running through her, she said, "Hey. I thought you were going to get some sleep." Something she could use herself.

"I will, but I just overheard an interesting conversation between Brandon Drake and some guy named Perry."

"Where?"

"The mass grave."

"What the heck was Brandon doing out there?" And with Ned Perry, of all people.

"Something I wondered myself. This Perry guy wanted to know who owned the land."

"I heard he's been bugging people about it," Lexie said, gazing onto the bay whose shore was barely dotted with large houses and mansions, keeping the area from being overpopulated. "He can't get anyone else to sell him shoreline land so I guess he figures that since that land has partial access to the water, he could build his development there."

A shiver shot through her. If Ned succeeded in finding the owner and convinced him to sell, would future condo buyers be warned they were going to be living over a former mass grave?

Simon broke into her thoughts. "That's not actually why I called, though."

"What's up?"

"Brandon is hiding something."

"As in?"

"Don't know. But Perry was putting the squeeze on him."

"What kind of squeeze?"

"Blackmail."

"I don't believe it." Simon didn't respond and Lexie realized that he was serious. "You think it could be about Drake Enterprises involvement with the human trafficking?"

"What else?"

Lexie's stomach clenched. She didn't want to believe that Brandon had been involved or that he was hiding something to protect the family name. But as they had discussed earlier, Brandon had to be considered a suspect, along with Cliff and Doug Heller. She turned and gazed at the east wing again, the visible damage from the fire an immediate reminder that someone else had thought Brandon was involved with the human trafficking operation.

"All right," she said, then glanced around to make

sure no one was around to overhear. "I have the key with me. I'll see what I can find out."

The lighting team had arrived. They would create pools of light to accentuate particular areas of the ballroom—the fireplace, the trio of trees, the silent auction area, among others—plus they'd create a special effect so that it would seem as if it were snowing inside. The first thing they needed to do was to figure out the power situation in case they had to add a generator.

"Can we see the breaker boxes?" the older man named Rick asked.

Isabella had entered the room and Lexie waved the maid over. "Rick needs to check on the electrical situation. Can you show him where the breakers are?"

Isabella gave her a sour expression, but said, "This way," and moved off, Rick and his young assistant following.

The high school kids arrived, and Lexie got them started decorating the already-lit balsam trees with white icicles and red and gold ornaments.

Another crew arrived with the tables and chairs. Food service would be confined to two other public rooms—the reception parlor for the buffet and the grand dining room for eating the festive meal. Lexie handed them computer printouts that showed how to set up the myriad tables.

Everyone was hard at work, and everything

seemed to be going smoothly. Lexie relaxed a little, certain all would be ready in time for the ball the next evening.

Good, because she had some snooping to do.

Brandon had been gone when she arrived and Marie had left the house to run some errands, so there was no time like the present.

With her unlimited access to Drake House, Lexie could move through any of the rooms in the public wing without raising suspicions. When Marie had turned over the key to her, she'd said it didn't fit any of the doors in the house, but she had probably just checked the key against the room doors, not against the furniture.

Lexie started with the first-floor rooms she'd been hired to decorate and checked for locked cabinets. No luck until she found a buffet with a drawer with a lock. Unfortunately, the key barrel was too big to insert.

She strolled through the kitchen, which at the moment was empty. Did she dare check out the rooms Marie's father had used before his death, which now were occupied by the housekeeper?

Lexie's hand was on the door handle when she heard a noise behind her and whirled around guiltily.

Shelley Zachary had just come from one of the back rooms used for laundry and storage. The house-keeper was balancing a tray filled with crystal serving dishes that she put on a stainless steel counter.

"Can I help you with something, Lexie?"

"I was looking for you, actually," Lexie lied, her heart thundering. "I just wondered if you knew when Marie was going to be back."

Shelley's narrow face pulled tight and her penciled eyebrows rose, making her look suspicious. "Why don't you just call her on her cell?"

"I tried." Lexie hated lying and wasn't very good at it. She only hoped her voice sounded steady and convincing. "Signal's not going through or something."

Shelley stared at her for a moment, then started moving the crystal serving pieces from the tray to the counter. "I imagine Marie will be here within the hour. Not that I keep track of her comings and goings."

While Lexie said, "Thank you, Shelley," she was aware that the housekeeper was keeping track of everything that went on in this house. And in town. According to Marie, the housekeeper was quite a gossip. "Back to work," she said softly as if to herself.

She felt Shelley's eyes follow her to the ballroom door.

Shaking off the feeling undoubtedly caused by her own guilt, Lexie reconnoitered. She knew the second-floor parlors overlooking the ballroom had only a few tables and seating arrangements, so she didn't need to check them.

Entering the empty foyer, she hesitated before going upstairs, to the third-floor rooms Marie and

Brandon were using until the roof and other damage to the east wing was repaired. If she was to go up there, she needed a plausible explanation to cover her furtive actions.

Then it came to her. She grabbed extra greenery and a couple of plants that hadn't been set out yet. If anyone saw her, she could say she was simply spreading some of the Christmas cheer to her best friend's private quarters. Halfway up the staircase, she felt the small hairs at the back of her neck tickle and got a weird feeling that made her stomach do a flip. Had Shelley Zachary followed her from the kitchen? Though she glanced down, Lexie saw no one in the foyer.

She was probably feeling weird because of her friendship with Marie and therefore with Brandon.

What would her friend think if she caught Lexie in her private quarters and didn't buy the decorating excuse? Pulse humming, she rushed up to the third floor. Surely Marie would believe her cover story, especially since she planned to spruce up the sitting room.

Lexie hadn't been up here since she was a kid. She and Marie used to explore the house and play hide-and-seek and other games in the big rooms. Then one day Edwin had caught them. Marie's father had been very big on propriety and had told them they were quite out of line going where they weren't invited. She'd been scared straight then, but now thinking back on it, Lexie wondered if he hadn't been secretly amused…

She entered the sitting room first, placed the gerbera daisies on the side table next to the sofa and the mums on a table between two chairs before the fireplace. After arranging the greenery on the mantel, she went back to her real purpose. She found only one lock on the cabinet holding crystal glasses and pitchers and bottles of liquor. The key proved too large for the opening.

Getting that feeling again, like interested eyes were following her, Lexie rechecked the foyer, thinking that if someone spotted her, she would have to give up the search and go back downstairs.

The foyer was clear. But not her sense of being watched. Guilt certainly put her imagination on overdrive.

Shaking away the unsettling feeling, she continued her search.

No furniture in the bedroom Marie and Brandon were now sharing required a key. Thankfully, Lexie thought, not wanting to invade her friend's privacy any more than she had to.

In the rear of the wing, there were a couple of storerooms, one for linens, the other filled with boxes. Nothing that required a key in either.

Relieved, Lexie was about to return to work

downstairs when she realized she needed to check the east wing, as well. Doing so might be dangerous. She didn't know how extensive the damage was or how safe entering those rooms would be. But she couldn't let it go unsearched.

The sense of being watched followed her down the stairs and across the gallery as she moved from one wing to the other, but no matter how intensely she searched for prying eyes, she saw no one, nothing out of place.

The damage was worst in the rear where the roof had collapsed. The fire had started in the second-floor nursery. Lexie couldn't check that room, the one adjacent or above it, but she figured she could manage the rest. Even though she started at the front of the wing, she was more aware of the smoke damage than she was down in the ballroom, despite the clean-up crew that Brandon had brought in. She guessed the wing would need a new roof and possibly some new walls and flooring before the smell would be obliterated.

Just being in this part of the house now gave Lexie the creeps and she asked herself why she was doing this. Because she wanted to eliminate Brandon as a suspect and this was the only way she could do that. She kept thinking about the dead man who'd set fire to the east wing out of a need for revenge. He must have had some reason to suspect

Brandon. Maybe he'd found something…something that, should she find it, as well, would lead *her* to the real killer.

That decided, she got to work.

An antique cabinet in a parlor had a lock, as did a walnut armoire in what she assumed was Brandon's bedroom. Neither was a match to the key. She used the side stairs to get to the third floor, but stopped halfway up when she realized she was putting herself in physical danger. So she headed back down and continued investigating the abandoned first-floor rooms. No better luck there.

Soon, there was only one room left that she could get at, other than Shelley's new quarters. Brandon's office sat directly in plain sight of the foyer.

Just as she thought it, the entry door opened and Marie came in, carrying several packages. Before her friend could see her, Lexie backed up and around a corner to avoid the other woman, who headed directly upstairs. Thankfully, she hadn't done so while Lexie was up there.

Waiting a minute to make certain the coast was clear, Lexie approached the door to the office. Just to play it safe, she knocked. Perhaps Brandon had returned and was sequestered in there.

No answer.

Even so, her pulse was racing as she tried the handle. It turned easily. She slipped inside, pulling the door closed behind her before feeling for the light switch.

Brandon's office looked just as it must have when his grandfather had first furnished it. The floor was covered with an old Oriental carpet and the furniture—serpentine partners' desk with leather top, chest of file drawers with marquetry detail and matching credenza—were all of mahogany with brass accents, including locks.

Lexie tried the desk first. The lock on the middle drawer was old-fashioned, the kind that would take a key like the one found on the grounds. She tried to slip the key in the lock, but it didn't quite fit.

She moved to the cabinet with file drawers and her pulse sped up as did her breath when she noticed that the leaf pattern in the veneer trim matched the pattern at the end of the key. Taking a deep breath, she inserted the key into the lock. It slipped in easily, but didn't turn. The fit was close enough, however, for her to believe that her key would fit a similar cabinet.

Undoubtedly, the cabinets had been bought by the same Drake—Brandon's grandfather Henry. The matching file cabinet then would most likely be found in one of the Drake Enterprises offices.

Lexie had just taken the key from the lock when she realized she wasn't alone. Palming the key, she turned to face Isabella.

"Can I help you with something?" Isabella asked as if she were the mistress of the house rather than the maid.

Considering that she hadn't brought any plants or decorations into the office, Lexie figured she couldn't use that as an excuse, so she said the first thing that came to mind. "I lost something yesterday and thought it might be in here."

"Hmm, I don't remember your being in Brandon's office yesterday."

Lexie raised her eyebrows. Isabella did have an inflated sense of self-importance.

"I didn't realize you were keeping track of my every move."

Isabella ignored the dig. "I can help you look for whatever it is you lost."

"That won't be necessary."

"No trouble."

"You have more important things to do."

"Not at the moment."

"Then perhaps you should ask Marie for something to do."

"I don't work for Marie."

Getting more irritated with Isabella by the second, Lexie said, "Then find something else to do...away from here."

Finally Isabella backed down and gave her a sulky expression before leaving the room. Lexie sagged against the desk and slipped the key into her back pocket.

She had more than one reason to be relieved. While she couldn't say for certain that Brandon was innocent, the fact that she couldn't open his file drawer with the key meant it belonged to a different if matching cabinet, one that undoubtedly would be found at the Drake Enterprises offices.

And the person really in charge of the business was Doug Heller…

Chapter Eight

"Your daughter's on the move, Mr. Shea," the body-guard assigned to watch Katie informed Simon.

A call from Bray Sloane having woken him up a short while ago, Simon was getting ready to go into town to meet the man. "With whom?"

"Alone. She's on foot. Looks like she's heading for Main Street."

"I'm ready to leave now," Simon said, shrugging into his leather jacket. "I'll be in Jenkins Cove in ten. Call me back when you know where Katie's going."

"Will do."

Simon shoved the cell in his inner jacket pocket, grabbed his car keys and left the fishing shack. He pulled on his gloves as he ran to the truck, which he'd parked on the other side of the camp, since again there had been no patrol car parked at the mass gravesite.

A sense of excitement filled him as he clambered into the truck, put on his sunglasses and a brimmed hat. The day was as bright as his sudden change in mood.

He couldn't help himself. Couldn't keep himself from grinning.

Katie…his daughter…

He still had trouble fathoming that he'd fathered a child. A child he would finally get to see in a few minutes. Not just a photo like the one of her and Lexie, but Katie herself. Not that he would actually introduce himself. He just wanted to get a look at her, even if from afar.

He started the truck and edged out of the stand of trees and headed for town.

For so many years, he'd been without family. He was an only child. His mother died when he was still a kid and his father was usually too drunk to know he existed, other than to make his life miserable. Once Rufus Shea had loved him—Simon was sure of that—but it was as if he'd blamed Simon for his wife's death. That's when his father's drinking had gone from social to serious. That's when Simon's home life had collapsed.

How desperately he'd been looking forward to starting his own family with Lexie that Christmas Eve thirteen years ago. Unbeknownst to him, he had. Sort of. If Katie wasn't aware that he was her dad—if he wasn't allowed to know her, to influence her as she grew into a lovely young lady—did his having fathered her count?

He would take what he could get. When this was over, he wouldn't deserve more.

His cell rang when he was about a minute from town. The ID told him it was the bodyguard.

"So where is she?"

"Katie headed straight into the supermarket. Just went inside. Do you want me to take off when you get here?"

"Not at all. I just want to see her for myself, you know, so that I can be sure she's okay. And then I have a meeting with your boss."

"Bray's in town?"

"He will be shortly. You keep an eye on my girl. Don't let anything happen to her."

"Check."

Simon drove past the bodyguard's car on the street across from Jenkins Cove Market and pulled into the parking lot. His pulse ticked faster as he left the car and went inside, still wearing the dark glasses and hat so that he wouldn't be recognized…if anyone still remembered him after all these years.

Christmas music blasted him as he grabbed a cart and raced down the aisles, looking for Katie. He found her in the aisle with baking goods. She was just putting a bag of sugar in her cart. Slowing, he pretended to be looking for something when he really was checking out his daughter. She was beautiful, a young Lexie. He couldn't stop looking at her.

She was tall for twelve—maybe five-six—and slender. Her short, dark hair was fashionably spiked, but her face was free of makeup, leaving her with a clear complexion and natural color in her cheeks. She looked up and even from a distance, he could see the clear green of her large round eyes.

His eyes.

Apparently sensing that he'd been watching her, Katie froze and gave him a weird look. Not wanting to freak her out, he picked something off the shelf, threw it in his cart and headed for the checkout.

As he passed her, from the corner of his eye, Simon saw Katie move away slightly. Damn! He hadn't meant to scare her. He'd just wanted a close-up look at his daughter without her having to know who he was, and now he'd ruined it. He fought the urge to look back at her.

"Will that be all, sir?" The kid at the register raised his voice to be heard over the piped-in Christmas music.

Simon grunted and looked down to see what he'd thrown in his cart. Cherry pie filling. "Yeah," he muttered, placing the can on the counter and pulling out his wallet.

As much as he wanted to glance back, to see what Katie was doing, he kept his focus where it belonged.

His heart hurt for the years they'd missed. Surely there was some way he could be in his daughter's life. He was already regretting severing his relationship with his own father. He should have tried to help the old man get over his alcoholism instead of running out on him.

If he had, he would never have been forced to fight in a war he'd wanted no part of, would have a totally different life now.

On the way out of the market, Simon spotted a Christmas food drop for needy families and added the cherry pie filling to the cans and boxes already there. And then he kept going, to the lot, to his truck, never once looking back just in case Katie was there.

He headed straight for the diner at the east end of town in hopes that there would be fewer people who might recognize him. The place wasn't fancy, though there were Christmas lights in the window and a small tree near the register. Bray was in a back booth waiting for him. Simon waved, but stopped at the counter where a redheaded waitress with a big name tag identifying her as Wanda was giving one of the customers his check.

He got her attention. "Morning, Wanda. I could use coffee and breakfast if you're still serving it."

"We're still serving it, sugar. What's your pleasure?"

"The works. Surprise me. I'm about hungry enough to eat a snake."

"We serve snakes here, but we don't feed snakes to our customers." She laughed at her own joke and poked her head through the window to the kitchen to order a breakfast. "Hey, Sam, one Lumberjack!"

His stomach already growling, Simon moved to the table and gave the big man there the once-over. His dark hair was spiked, his gray eyes seemingly free of the nightmares they'd once reflected, his body muscular.

"Bray." He held out his hand and the other man stood to take it. They were of equal height and strength. "It's been a long time."

"A lot of years," Bray agreed.

They both sat as Wanda arrived with Simon's coffee. "Brought you boys a pot," she said, setting it in the middle of the table and a mug in front of Simon. "That breakfast will be up in a few minutes."

"My stomach's already growling," Simon told her. Then, when she left, he turned to Bray. Before he'd left Afghanistan, Bray had been a mess. His eyes had held that look identifying him as a man on the verge of a breakdown. Not anymore. Simon would bet Bray's wife, Claire, had everything to do with that. "Good to see you."

"If only the circumstances were better," Bray said, keeping his voice low.

"Hopefully, when I'm done with this town, they will be." But did he want to be done with the town if that meant he was done with Lexie and Katie? Did he want to take the kind of revenge that would push them away forever? Not wanting to complicate things right at the moment, Simon focused on the reason for the meeting. "So what do you have for me?"

"Claire got a response to her ad. A Hans Zanko claims to be one of the survivors. He's in Annapolis, not too far from the Five Star Security offices." Bray handed Simon a folder. "Do you want Claire to follow up and interview him about what happened? He wants to be paid $10,000 for the information. He checks out as far as we can tell, but of course there aren't any records to prove his claim that he was brought over for his kidney. He could be in it for the money."

"That what you think?" When Bray shrugged, Simon opened the folder to find a photo and contact info for a man who looked to be in his forties.

"He didn't send that photo, by the way. Claire got it off the Internet."

Which seemed to legitimize Hans Zanko, though Simon was still uncertain. "I would have guessed they would pick someone younger to be a donor. Like in his twenties, not forties."

"Except we don't know how long ago the operation started. Some of those bodies they've dug up from the mass grave go way back. This guy has been in the country for a dozen years at least."

"I'll check it out myself. If this Zanko is legit, I may be able to get more out of him, since I do have something in common with him. You just get me the cash from the account as soon as you get back to the office." Simon had put $25,000 at Bray's disposal for expenses and could move money into the account electronically. "And thank your wife for this."

"I'll do that. I know you're in an odd situation, what with everyone thinking you're dead and all. You might need some backup other than from me. Someone in the system."

"A lawyer?"

"A cop. A detective for the state police. *The* detective, actually."

"You mean the one investigating the victims…the mass grave site?" When Bray nodded, Simon asked, "How do you know him?"

"He's my brother-in-law, Rand McClellan. He's good. He's fair. And he knows that things aren't always what they seem," Bray said, his tone odd enough that Simon took notice. "He can keep things under wraps until the time is right."

"I'll think about it. So why did you really want to see me?" Simon asked. "You could have sent me Zanko's photo and contact information. You could have told me about your brother-in-law in a phone conversation."

"Well, uh…"

"C'mon, Bray, what gives?"

"I only hesitate because you might find this hard to believe," Bray began. "My former partner at Five Star Security and I had a contract with a scientific company working for DARPA. There was a lab accident—an experiment that was aimed at developing a new biochemical warfare weapon. It left me without my memory for a while…" Bray looked around as if making sure no one could overhear. "…and gave me an ability I didn't have before."

"What kind of ability?"

"I can, uh…when I touch something, I can see something that happened to the object in the past. If I touch something connected to the murders—that key you told me about—maybe I can give you a lead that'll help."

Simon didn't immediately respond. He was wondering if his old acquaintance was in as good a condition as he'd first believed. Bray spoke up again. "Let me show you how it works. Give me something of yours and I'll tell you what I see."

Simon thought about it for a moment and pulled out his wallet. From it, he took a flat piece of metal with a picture of a crab. It had once been a pin, but cheaply put together, it had come apart. Still, Simon hadn't been able to get rid of the souvenir.

He handed it to Bray and watched the other man's forehead pull into a frown of concentration.

"A carnival of some sort…food…corn on the cob…crabs…"

"You could get that from the picture."

"A ring tossing game…a young woman…long bare legs…dark hair in a ponytail…big smile. She's determined to win…"

Suddenly Simon saw it all again—him and Lexie at the Eastern Shore Crabfest, the day he'd fallen head over heels for her. He'd loved her ever since they were kids, but this one perfect day in August with her had made him see what life could be like if they could spend it together. It had made him want something he'd never had.

The day had been magic. *Lexie* had been magic. She'd cast a spell on him. So when she'd won the ring toss and had insisted on giving him her prize, the pin had taken on a value far above its true worth.

I'll keep this forever, Lexie. No matter where I am, it'll remind me of you.

Simon still remembered his exact words. And he'd been true to his vow. He'd kept the pin, had taken it out to feel closer to home—to her—even in war.

"She won the game and gave you the pin," Bray

said, seeming as if he were coming out of a trance. "And you said you would keep it forever."

Simon cursed under his breath, but before he could say anything, a platter landed on the table before him.

"Hope it'll do you," Wanda said.

A glance at the plate of pancakes and eggs and potatoes and bacon and sausage and toast was enough to make Simon's stomach growl.

But when Simon looked at Bray and said, "I hope it'll do me, too," he wasn't talking about the food.

Chapter Nine

"We're done for the day," Lexie told Marie late in the afternoon just after her crew had cleared out.

"You've really done a fabulous job on this place," Marie said. "Better than I even imagined."

Lexie glanced back into the ballroom and admitted that it did look pretty good, definitely the holiday wonderland her friend had requested. The scent of pine wafted from the room that now was unrecognizable in gold and red and green splendor. The lights weren't even on, nor the special snow effect, and still it was transformed into a fairy-tale setting.

In two days her mood had shifted as greatly as the ballroom had. The Grinch was hiding somewhere, chased away by a sense of expectancy.

But it wasn't the holiday that had gotten to her.

Being with Simon again had lifted her spirits, if only for the moment.

Knowing she couldn't share her secret with Marie

without betraying Simon's wishes, Lexie decided she'd better leave fast before she folded and gave it up.

"I'm glad you're pleased."

"I hope it lightens Brandon's mood," Marie said. "Something's been bothering him and he won't talk about it. Says it's business and he wants to forget about business when he's with me."

A curl of anxiety tightened Lexie's stomach. "That's good. Isn't it?"

"I guess." Marie shrugged. "Although I hate being shut out when I might be able to help him."

Lexie prayed that Brandon didn't know anything about the human trafficking operation. "I'm sure his mood will even out. Give him time to get used to your being around and believing he can share things with you."

"You're right."

Hoping she was, Lexie gave Marie a big hug. "See you tomorrow."

Lexie left and hurried out to the car. Brandon had to be innocent. Surely his mood had shifted because of some business pressures that had nothing to do with the horrific acts that had been going on in Jenkins Cove. If he was guilty or even knew something about the operation that he hadn't revealed to the authorities, Marie would be devastated.

Having gotten a call from Simon just as she was wrapping up for the afternoon, Lexie took off and headed for town to meet him at the diner. When she'd asked him what was up, however, he'd been all mysterious. She expected there was more than a fast dinner together involved. He must have gotten some information.

Halfway there, Lexie realized that the same vehicle had been behind her since she left the estate.

From a distance, it looked like it could be the same silver sedan that she'd seen that morning. Surely not. Surely her imagination was working overtime. Wanting to know for certain, Lexie slowed her SUV to let the other vehicle catch up. It slowed, as well.

Her pulse fluttered. What if someone really *was* following her? Her assailant?

She stepped on the gas, now wanting to get away from the car, but the other driver did the same, keeping the same distance between them, just far enough back so that she couldn't be sure of anything. If only it would get closer, she could use her cell to take a photo, maybe get a shot of the plates that could be blown up.

When she entered Jenkins Cove, she made a couple of unnecessary turns. The other vehicle did, as well. The car was close enough now that she could see that it was a silver sedan. Still too far away to get a good shot on her cell phone.

When she turned back on Main Street, Lexie stepped on the gas and headed straight for the diner where Simon was waiting for her. Parking the car right out front, she ran into the diner, pulling her cell from her pocket, then stared out the window, waiting for the car to pass.

It didn't.

"Lexie, over here."

Simon's voice pulled her attention from the window. She turned to see him sitting with another man at a back booth. How weird, considering he didn't want his presence known. After glancing back through the window, she joined them.

As she approached the booth, Simon frowned at her. "What's wrong, Lexie?"

"I think I'm being followed."

Simon and the stranger locked gazes, and getting a sick feeling in her stomach, Lexie sank down into the booth. "Why do I get the feeling you know something about this?"

"Because he's my man," the stranger said. "I'm Bray Sloane."

Lexie turned to Simon and couldn't keep the accusing tone out of her voice. "You decided to have me followed and didn't tell me?"

"He's a bodyguard," Simon told her, "doing what you wouldn't let *me* do. You agreed it would be a good idea to keep Katie safe."

"But you didn't say anything about hiring a body-guard for *me!*"

"You need protection, but I know you would have refused if I'd mentioned it."

"Apparently you know me well." She turned to Bray who sat in silence, but with a knowing expression.

"Tell your man his services won't be needed anymore."

"Don't tell him any such thing," Simon countered. "Unless..."

"Unless what?"

"You agree to let *me* protect you until the situation is resolved."

"You mean move in?" Lexie's pulse quickened but she said, "I don't want to confuse Katie."

As if Katie were the only one who would be confused by Simon's presence...

"You told me she was staying at her grandmother's for a few days."

"Yes, but then what?" Lexie asked. "What happens when she comes back home?"

"We can renegotiate...if the situation isn't resolved before then."

Lexie gritted her teeth. She knew Simon would insist that she have protection, no matter what she said. In truth, he was right. She'd been attacked twice. She definitely could see the advantage of someone watching her back. Part of her wanted it to be Simon himself. Though her feelings about him and about his staying away from her were ambiguous, she wanted the chance to sort them out. She simply didn't like someone else suddenly making decisions for her.

Not even a ghost.

Sighing, she finally said, "Fine. You can move in."

"Fine?" Simon's brows shot up, showing his surprise at her easy capitulation.

"But you sleep on the couch."

"Fine," Simon said again, then turned to Bray. "Take the bodyguard off Lexie, but not off Katie."

"Will do."

Not liking being manipulated, Lexie took a big breath before asking, "So what did you want to see me about?"

Simon gave a quick look around the room before asking in a low voice, "The key. You have it on you, right?"

"What about it?"

"Bray would like to see it."

Lexie looked from Simon, to Bray, back to Simon again. "Why?" Did he think Bray would recognize it?

"Trust me. Just hand it over."

Lexie fished the key out of her back pocket and held it out to Bray. He took it from her and his head jerked slightly. His gaze locked on the key, he sat frozen.

"What—"

Simon's kick under the table stopped her from finishing. Bray was obviously in some kind of trance. His pale gray eyes had gone kind of weird, like they were in some other place. Her pulse sped up and she held her breath until he seemed to snap out of it enough to speak.

"The key fits an old file drawer," Bray said, his expression intent. "The drawer is part of a wood cabinet with leaves embossed in the trim."

Lexie started. He was describing the cabinet she'd found in Brandon's office.

"Someone is unlocking it…a man, from the hands. He's sorting through the files… Wait, he's stopping, pulling one out…Lala Falat."

Lexie started. Seeing Bray's eyes come back into focus as if he'd just come out of a trance, she said, "Lala Falat is one of the women whose kidney was taken. She died later, of complications." And her fiancé had plotted revenge against Brandon. "Did you see any of the other names?"

"A few. Anna Bencek…Franz Dobra…Tomas Elizi… That's it, I'm afraid."

"The face?" Lexie asked. "Did you see the man's face?"

Bray shook his head. "I saw through his eyes, just as if I were the man in question. Sorry I can't give you more, that's just how it works."

He handed back the key.

Lexie might have disbelieved Bray if he hadn't described the cabinet so accurately.

"So what do we do with this information?" she asked Simon.

"See if those other names are of people who survived."

A QUARTER OF AN HOUR LATER, Simon squared the check with the waitress and gave her a big tip.

"Nice waiting on you, honey," Wanda said, obviously pleased. "You come back any time."

"I was never here," Simon said, handing her another bill.

Her eyebrows shot up but she didn't miss a beat. "Never saw you before, stranger."

When the waitress left, Bray rose from the booth. "Nice to meet you, Lexie."

"Thanks for your help."

Simon took another look at the names he'd written down—those Bray had picked up from the folders in his vision, as well as the one who'd contacted Claire. Trying to track down these people was someplace to start, even if he had to pay for information that could lead him to the truth. He certainly could afford it. And he would start trying to reach any survivors as soon as he moved his things into Lexie's house.

As they left the diner, Simon stuffed the list in his pocket and said, "We need to stop at the fishing cabin before going to your place."

"You can meet me there."

"And let you out of my sight? Not a good idea. Not part of the deal."

"Surely you don't think I agreed to have you shadow my every movement."

"Only the ones that could get you into trouble. Truth is, my instincts tell me to get you the hell out of here. You and Katie."

"That's not going to happen."

"I can make it happen, Lexie. And I will if I have to…if you don't cooperate."

He could see that Lexie was still fighting the idea, that she didn't like being told what to do, but in the end she nodded. "All right."

She led their little procession straight to the fishing camp, while he followed close enough that no one could get between them.

He wondered if he was doing the wrong thing getting so personally involved with her again. Yes, he loved her, yes, part of him wanted to think there was a way he could have some kind of life with her and Katie in it. But the other part of him—the dark part, fostered in a country halfway across the world—wanted revenge for what had happened to him, and he wasn't certain which emotion was stronger. He wasn't certain he would be good for Lexie or for their daughter, not only because of his past, but because of his planned future.

If Lexie knew the kinds of things he'd been forced to do—the kinds of things he would like to do to repay whoever had set him up—he couldn't imagine that she'd want him in her life. Certainly not in Katie's. But after the life he'd been coerced into, how could he let go of the past until he'd seen that justice was served?

Five minutes at the fishing camp and they were off again. Though Lexie's remote home had made her more susceptible to her assailant, the place had its advantages. No one would know that Simon was there.

Once he got his stuff inside and made sure the premises were safe, Simon moved his truck into the wooded area where he'd parked before. Then he jogged back to the house.

Lexie was standing at the kitchen door, watching for him through the window. Simon's heart began to jog faster than his legs. With her dark hair spilling around her pale face, her expression at once worried and welcoming, she was a sight any man would be glad to come home to. He just didn't think that man could be him.

"I put some coffee on," she said after opening the door to let him inside. "If you could drink another cup."

"I can live on coffee." He didn't tell her there were times when he had, when in the field food had run out and they'd used coffee grounds a second and third time to have something warm to drink at night.

"So where do we start?"

"Computer. I'm going to do searches on all four names, see what I come up with."

"You mean addresses?"

"And telephone numbers. And hopefully other information, as well. The more we have, the better off we'll be."

"I can help you with that. I have my laptop here."

Then he told her about Bray's wife getting a response from a possible survivor named Hans Zanko.

"He wants to sell you information? What about justice?"

Simon shrugged. "Justice wouldn't pay the bills or feed his family. Who knows his circumstances? He might never have really recovered from what they did to him."

As he himself hadn't recovered, Simon thought. *Maybe he never would.*

"Well, I still think it's horrible." Lexie poured two mugs of coffee and handed one to him. "Let's get started with that research."

Sitting at the kitchen table, Simon worked on his laptop, while Lexie worked on hers. Good thing she had installed a home networking system. Simon had found his wi-fi to be fairly useless when he'd been at the fishing camp, but it worked great here.

He started with Franz Dobra, she with Tomas Elizi.

Simon found a Frank Dobra. When he called the

number and explained why he was calling, the woman at the other end agreed that her husband's name really was Franz, but everyone called him Frank. She also said that he'd left her for some floozy and she had no clue where to find him. Then she hung up on him.

The only Tomas Elizi Lexie found was in Europe.

"I don't know if it's me or if he simply doesn't exist," Lexie said. "He could have changed his name, moved like your Frank/Franz Dobra did."

"Or he might not have made it," Simon said, thinking of the bodies from the mass grave that might never be identified.

"Or that."

Trying not to be discouraged, Simon said, "I'll get hold of Hans Zanko and set something up. At least he's willing to talk. Claire got his cell number."

"Okay, I'll start a search on Anna Bencek."

Simon pulled out his cell and hit paydirt when the man immediately answered, "Zanko here."

"Mr. Zanko, I'm the one interested in getting information on the human trafficking operation run out of Jenkins Cove."

"I would be happy to speak with you in person. What did you say your name was?"

"I didn't. It's Madison. Jake Madison." Until he was ready, Simon wasn't about to give out his real name to anyone, not even to a survivor.

A heavy pause was followed by Zanko saying, "All right, Mr. Madison. You can meet me at an abandoned boatyard near Annapolis at nine this evening." He gave Simon the address. "And don't forget your part of the bargain."

"Don't worry, I'll bring the money."

By the time Simon hung up, Lexie had had some luck.

"An Anna Bencek has a dress shop in Easton. Here's the address and phone number."

Surprised that she'd possibly located a survivor so close, Simon immediately followed up, but was met with a recording. He hung up. "She's out to lunch or something. Let's go meet Bray to get that money. We can stop in Easton on the way to Annapolis. Hopefully, we can catch the Bencek woman."

Chapter Ten

They left a short while later, Simon driving Lexie's SUV. On edge, she kept a sharp eye on the sideview mirror, but saw no one following them. Not until they were on the road heading north to Easton did she allow herself to relax. The drive was all too short.

They went directly to the Dover Shopping Center where a Christmas carol blared out over the lot. The dress shop was at the far end. As they approached the store on foot, Lexie looked at the holiday window display. Another reminder of the day both of their lives had changed forever. But for some reason, it didn't bother her as much as it might have mere days ago.

Simon opened the door and placed his hand on Lexie's back to guide her inside. His touch made her catch her breath, so she quickly put some distance between them. She had to keep her mind on their mission, not on Simon himself. A look around revealed one woman looking at a display of accessories, another sorting through a rack of dresses.

A too-thin, midthirties blonde came from the back with a purse in hand. "I find it."

The customer at the accessory display immediately joined her and bought the purse. As she left the store, the woman who'd been browsing through the dresses walked out, as well, leaving Lexie and Simon alone with the owner.

"Can I help?" she asked them with a big smile, her words tinged with a faint accent reminiscent of Eastern Europe.

"Anna Bencek?" Simon asked.

"Yes." Her smile wavered a little and caution reflected from her pale blue eyes.

"My name is Simon Shea and this is Lexie Thornton…from Jenkins Cove."

The smile disappeared altogether. "What you want with me?"

"Who are you afraid of?" Simon asked.

"I—I don't understand." The woman's hands shook slightly as she looked away from them and straightened a display. "If you don't make purchase, please leave. I—I close up now."

"Simon may have come on a bit strong," Lexie said, her voice soothing. "We mean you no harm, Ms. Bencek. We're hoping you can help us."

"To find dress?" Her voice was stronger now. Angry.

Simon said, "No—"

Lexie touched Simon's arm and gave him a look that said, *Let me handle this.* "We need information…about the people who brought you to this country and hurt you."

The Bencek woman shook her head. "You leave now."

Taking his cue from Lexie, Simon softened his approach. "Please. They hurt me, too. They took me from my home across an ocean, just as they did to you. They didn't take my kidney, but they put me to work as a soldier in a war I'd only heard about, and all because I saw a young man murdered. A young man who was trying to escape them, maybe even someone you knew. I was held prisoner for years. And now I want to find out who was responsible."

"I—I can tell you nothing."

Did she mean she couldn't identify anyone or that she didn't know if she should help them? Lexie sensed Simon's frustration.

"Please," Lexie said softly. "The people responsible for the human trafficking operation shouldn't get away with what they did. Maybe they'll do other terrible things. I'm sure you've heard about the mass grave—"

A choked sound came from the other woman and

she grasped her throat. "My friend Bernice...she disappeared...when I heard about bodies..."

Simon said, "Perhaps you could close up and we could go somewhere private?"

The shop owner resisted for a moment, and then she nodded. A few minutes later, they sat in the back room, a combination office and store-room filled with cartons. Anna Bencek sat in her desk chair, hands gripping the arms, while Simon took two chairs from a stack and set them down for him and Lexie.

"Anything you remember might be of help."

"Ten of us came to United States. We pay for passage and papers to work. When we get here, they say not enough money. Pay again. We have no money. So they say we pay with kidney or go back."

"How horrible," Lexie murmured.

"How *did* you get here?" Simon asked.

"Boat...cargo ship. We have cots below. People sick. They gave medicine. We sleep. Then one day, they tell us we are here. No port. Only water."

"They transferred you to a smaller boat?"

She nodded. "A yacht."

Lexie stiffened. "A yacht...a sailing yacht?"

"No sails, motor. Big yacht."

"The name—did you see it?" Simon asked.

Again, the woman nodded. "I never forget. *Drake's Passage.*"

Feeling sick, Lexie half tuned out as Simon continued to question the woman.

"Where did the yacht take you?"

"To warehouse where we wait like jail. Then to place for surgery, then back to warehouse for a few days until is okay to go."

Lexie was only vaguely aware of Simon's further questions and the fact that Anna Bencek had nothing further of value to tell them.

When he was done, they thanked the woman and headed for Annapolis and Five Star Security, where Simon was going to collect the money to pay Hans Zanko for information.

"So what do you think?" he asked as they got on the road.

Lexie swallowed hard before saying, "*Drake's Passage* is owned by Drake Enterprises."

Now there was no doubt Cliff or Doug Heller was involved. Brandon just couldn't be…

"So is Brandon into boating?" Simon asked.

"No…no!"

"Why the emphasis?"

"He didn't do it. I told you the key didn't fit the file drawers of his cabinet."

"I assume he has keys to the corporate offices."

"I suppose so," she said grudgingly.

"And access to the yacht."

Lexie sighed. "He used it a couple of times last

spring and summer. I know because he ordered fresh flowers for the cruises. Something about a thank-you to big contributors to the Drake Foundation. That's a far cry from importing illegals for their kidneys. After his wife, Charlotte, died, I thought it was odd that Brandon continued the practice, because he became something of a recluse…"

"And there's the matter of Perry trying to black-mail him," Simon reminded her. "So we can't elimi-nate him as a suspect, after all. The three men who would have access to the yacht are Brandon and Cliff and Doug Heller. Right?"

Lexie didn't argue. She had no proof of Brandon's innocence. Instead, she sank into a de-pressed silence.

BRAY WAS WAITING for them at the front counter of Five Star Security in an Annapolis strip mall. "The money's in the office. Do you need backup?" he asked Simon.

"Probably not a good idea if I don't want to scare the guy off."

Simon hugged Lexie to him as they followed Bray down a hallway to an office. She leaned in to his side and her pulse suddenly accelerated. She wanted him to hold her this way forever, but she knew that was highly unlikely. She would take what she could get.

Bray led them to a desk and picked up a small leather case. "All hundreds."

"Thanks, man." Simon took the case and shook Bray's hand.

"Anything else you need," Bray said, "just call."

"Will do."

With that, they left, Lexie wondering if they were crazy. Shouldn't they just leave this whole investigation to the police? She wanted to say so, but she didn't dare. Simon was on a mission and he had the chops and the skills to pull it off. If she tried to divert him from his course, he would simply leave her behind.

Again...

Still, when they arrived at the abandoned boatyard and got out of the SUV, Lexie felt a cold lump settle in the pit of her stomach. No other vehicle was in sight.

She didn't like the creepy feeling the place gave her, nor the location or the fact that the area wasn't lit. Still, the moon was bright enough for her to see hulls of boats in all states of decomposition and rust in the weed-strewn land all the way to the waterline. A couple more boats stuck out of the water near a collapsed pier. Added to the derelicts were a graffiti-covered building half-collapsed on one side, two abandoned cars and something that looked like a horse trailer.

Why had Zanko wanted to meet them here?

The place was surrounded by a chain-link fence, but parts of it seemed to have crumpled to half the original six-foot height. Simon vaulted over the fence with ease, then reached out and helped her over it, too.

Lexie landed against Simon's chest and his arms snaked around her back. Her heartbeat sped up, but she wasn't sure if it was because of Simon or because of the hairs rising at the back of her neck. She didn't like this place—not at all. Breathless, she pushed away from him.

"So where is he?" she gasped, looking around wildly when she heard a sharp crack.

Even as dirt at her feet churned, Simon threw himself on her and pushed her to the ground, then rolled her into the shadow of one of the derelict boats. More shots rang out and wood splintered.

"Why is he firing at us?" Lexie whispered. "Does he think you're one of the bad guys?"

"No." Simon reached inside his jacket and pulled out a handgun. "I think *he* is."

"What do you mean?"

The moon bathed Simon in its silver-blue glow, and Lexie could see his face clearly. Her heart thumped against her ribs and her mouth went dry. His expression was so hard, he was unrecognizable.

He looked nothing like the man she loved.

"STAY HERE," Simon ordered, getting into a crouch.

"You're not going to leave me here alone?"

"I'm going to get him before he gets us." Something he was proficient at.

"Get him? You don't mean kill him?"

Hearing the horror in Lexie's question, Simon didn't answer. "Stay. Don't so much as poke your head out to see what's going on until I give you the all clear."

With that, he scrambled to the next wreck and then to the next. It took Zanko that long to realize he'd moved. A couple more shots followed. Simon was able to figure out that they came from what was left of the building. He was close and yet so far. If he didn't distract the man before making his run, he would be an easy target.

Looking around, Simon spotted what looked like a piece of loose board behind him. He snagged it with his foot and edged it up a little at a time so that it didn't leave the protective shadow of the hull. Finally, he was able to fully grasp it in his hand. A deep breath and he was ready. First he flung the board as far as he could to the other side of where Lexie still hid, then he ran.

Gunfire hit wood and metal in that opposite direction, but stopped just as Simon got to the outside wall of the building. He pressed his back against the boards and adjusted his breathing the way he'd learned so that Zanko wouldn't hear him. Barely a yard away, the opening that had once held a door awaited him.

Movement from the wreck where he'd left Lexie made him want to curse aloud. She was going to come after him. Damn it! He had to get Zanko before the bastard could get her! The supposed survivor would kill her, if he could. He would kill them both. They'd been set up by whoever had been running the operation, and Zanko—if that was even his real name—had been hired to get rid of them.

Simon threw himself through the doorway and rolled. Shots chewed up the flooring around him, but he got behind a collapsed table unscathed.

"You might as well give up now," he said. "If the man who hired you told you anything about me, you know I was trained by the best. Your life for a name."

In response, he earned a curse and another round of gunfire that pinned his location for Simon. He didn't want to kill the man—Zanko couldn't talk if he was dead—but he would if he had to, if it meant saving his own or Lexie's life.

Tuning into the night, Simon caught every sound, would be able to see every movement, no matter that the space was dark but for the faint moonlight cutting through the doorway and the glassless windows. He remained still, his breathing easy and shallow, but his quarry didn't have the same training. Zanko was making slight movements, probably looking for a way to get to Simon. His clothing rustled. He expelled his breath in little puffs of anxiety.

Simon shoved his gun in its holster and grabbed the legs of the table sheltering him. His muscles coiled in expectation and when the man made his move, so did Simon, lifting the table and using it as a shield as he plunged forward and smacked the other man hard.

"Aak!" Zanko jerked backward, the gun flying out of his hand and hitting something with a sharp thud.

Zanko was a big man, bigger than Simon, but definitely not as toned. Throwing what was left of the table to the side, Simon got his hands on the bastard and threw him, too, so that he hit a rotten support that broke with a sharp crack. The ceiling started sifting down on them, but that didn't stop Simon.

"Who hired you?" he demanded, ignoring the debris falling on him and dragging Zanko back up to his feet.

Eyes dark enough to look black in a puffy, beard-stubbled face glared at him. The man tried kneeing him, but Simon stepped to the side, at the same time catching Zanko's leg and twisting. Zanko rolled and flew into the wall, his arm punching through the rotting wood to the outside. He struggled to free himself, but didn't succeed until Simon grabbed the front of his jacket with both fists and gave a sharp pull.

"I don't intend to kill you," Simon growled. "But I intend to get a name from you."

Zanko spat and Simon ducked to the side, then twisted the other man's arm until he screamed.

"I was trained to get information from reluctant people," Simon said. "I know how to make you hurt, how to make you suffer. I don't even have to break anything to do it. I can even do it without leaving any mark on you." He had never tortured anyone, but Zanko didn't know that. "You can make things easier on yourself if you talk, Zanko. Give me the name of the man who hired you to kill us."

Just then Lexie slipped through the doorway and though Simon didn't so much as look her way, he sensed her, and the distraction of knowing she was there was enough to throw him off just a hair, just for a millisecond. Zanko struck out, gut-punching him this time, then hooking a foot behind Simon's knee and giving it a sharp tug. Simon went halfway down and though it only took seconds for him to recover, Zanko was on his way to the door.

Simon regained his footing too late. Zanko had already grabbed Lexie and spun around, using her as a shield.

"I, too, know how to make people hurt," he said,

his accent distinctly East Coast. "Don't move or I'll break something."

Simon's heart thudded hard against his ribs as Zanko backed out of the shack and Lexie's expression turned horrified as she tried to fight the man off. It was like watching a fly beating its wings against a predator. Simon thought fast, but he couldn't see a way of getting to Zanko without the bastard doing something nasty to Lexie.

"You can be sure that if you so much as cause her the slightest harm," Simon growled, "your life will be worthless, Zanko. I'll hunt you to the ends of the earth if I have to. I'll gut you and skin you and hang what's left of you out to dry!"

Zanko was backing Lexie down the beach now, toward the fallen pier. What the hell was he up to?

Though Simon followed, he didn't dare rush the man, lest he carry on with his threat against Lexie. He kept his distance, yet matched Zanko stride for stride.

Lexie wasn't stopping, either. She kept struggling in Zanko's arms, working her face over to his bare hand.

Knowing she was planning on biting the man, Simon whispered, "Don't do it, Lexie." But he knew she would and his muscles once more coiled for attack.

Suddenly, Zanko yelled, the sound cutting through the night. He lifted Lexie off her feet and tossed her as he might toss a piece of trash. Limbs flailing, she went flying at the broken wood of the downed pier. No contest about which of them to go after. Simon had to see to Lexie, to make certain she was all right.

In the water now, she was thrashing around in an attempt to free herself from the debris.

"I'm all right. Go after him!" she screamed.

But he was already reaching down to help her.

"Go!" Getting to her feet, she literally pushed him into moving.

Drawing his gun, Simon negotiated the pier, using it for cover in case Zanko had another piece. Then a motor cut through the night and Simon threw caution to the wind and raced around the wooden piles only to see a speedboat take off.

Simon aimed and took a couple shots, thinking to wound the man, maybe toss him out of the boat. But the motor revved and the speedboat practically went airborne.

Cursing, he lowered his gun even as Lexie joined him.

"Are you all right?" he asked.

"Shaken and maybe a little bruised is all."

Simon took her in his arms and held her, steady as rock. Inside he was shaking. He knew what atrocities humans could do to one another. Awful memories flickered through his mind like a photograph album from hell.

Though Lexie had gotten away relatively unscathed, the mere threat to her gave Simon one more reason to thirst for justice to be wielded by his own hand.

Chapter Eleven

As Simon drove back over the Bay Bridge toward Jenkins Cove, his threats against Zanko haunted Lexie, who had heard every chilling word.

They were just threats, she told herself, wrapping the blanket she luckily carried in the SUV more tightly around her. She was still wet from that dunk in the bay, but the dry cover and the heat blowing on her were keeping her warm enough physically.

It was her heart that had gone cold, and Lexie was trying to rationalize Simon's words.

He'd simply been trying to find a way to make Zanko talk, then to make certain the man didn't hurt her. But Lexie knew that wasn't really true, that there was a part of Simon that was damaged and downright scary. Not that *she* was threatened by him.

Even so, Simon scared her in a more visceral way.

Tonight had given her more of an idea of his experience as a mercenary. Had made her wonder if there was any coming back from that kind of psychological damage. Even though the choice to become a soldier for hire hadn't initially been his, he'd continued working for Shadow Ops and the CIA when he'd no longer had to.

Had Simon really felt he couldn't inflict himself on her—his excuse for staying away—or had that violent way of life become ingrained in him?

Simon had reason to be angry, to seek some kind of justice, but Lexie feared the only justice he really understood, really appreciated, was one linked to violence. A thought that made her shiver.

A fact that Simon noticed.

He broke the uneasy silence. "Lexie, are you sure you're all right? I can still get you to a clinic if there's any doubt."

They were about a mile from Jenkins Cove and all Lexie wanted to do was get home, get in the shower and then get into dry clothing.

"I'm fine. Just a little worse for wear, but I'll manage."

Simon went silent again, then, as they passed the diner where they'd met Bray, said, "You realize that we were set up, right?"

"It's pretty obvious, even to me."

"Which means whoever ran the human trafficking operation is onto us," he said. "That person must have caught the ad Claire ran, asking for any survivors to contact her. Zanko was the only one who did."

"But you don't think he's the one we've been looking for, do you?"

"He was a hired gun, Lexie, a professional. He may have been part of the operation. My instincts tell me what's left of it is bigger than one man. It couldn't just have been the three of them—the nameless head, the doctor and his assistant who hanged himself."

Lexie nodded. "Anna Bencek said ten people came to the United States together, too many for Dr. Janecek and Kreeger to handle by themselves."

"So it makes sense that they had help, whether from hired guns like Zanko or from other locals."

Locals—more people she knew. The thought left Lexie breathless.

"You're talking about the average person? You think just anyone might be involved?"

"Anyone who needs money and can use whatever is in it for him to clear his conscience."

Not wanting to think people she knew were guilty of propagating such horror, Lexie put it out of mind and thought again about the survivors, about what they'd learned and experienced that night.

"We should have known that no one who'd gone through what the survivors had been through would want to come forward voluntarily," Lexie said. "Zanko's asking for money made him more believable somehow." Remembering that Simon hadn't given away his name during their phone conversation, she asked, "But why would these people want to kill us when they didn't even know who we were?"

"They simply didn't care. The fact that anyone was onto them and was looking for information by finding survivors was enough. They couldn't chance our finding a real survivor who might talk."

Lexie's mind whirled with that thought. *Then what about the survivors themselves? Would the head of the operation get rid of any potential witnesses he could find?*

"Anna Bencek… Oh, no." A cold lump settled in Lexie's stomach. "What if we put her in danger?"

Simon cursed and immediately made a call on his cell. "Bray, we have a problem."

Simon then told Bray about the ambush that had been awaiting them and the possibility that someone could get to Anna Bencek.

Lexie sat stunned. She hadn't so much as guessed it would come to this. She'd never meant to put anyone else in danger, certainly not a woman who'd already been through so much. And she didn't want to be in danger again herself.

Three attacks in as many days were enough to send her running…but to where?

Her whole life was in Jenkins Cove.

Her business…her family…her daughter.

Wanting in the worst way to call Katie, to make

sure her daughter was safe, Lexie felt even more frightened and frustrated when she realized it was hours too late. Her parents went to bed early. If she called now, they would know something was wrong.

Closing his cell, Simon said, "Bray will put someone on it immediately. One of his men will keep an eye on the Bencek woman until this thing is settled."

"Thank God," Lexie said, still edgy. "I would never forgive myself if…" She forced herself to stop thinking that way. Anna Bencek would be all right. Bray's man would see to it. "Simon, can you call Katie's bodyguard? I just want to make sure she's all right."

"He would have called me if anything suspicious had happened, but if it'll make you feel better, of course I'll check."

He immediately made the second call just as they pulled into the driveway outside her house.

Lexie barely swallowed until Simon nodded at her and said, "Good," to the man at the other end. "We had some problems tonight. Be prepared, just in case." He hung up. "Lights went out about an hour ago. All is well at your parents' house."

"Thankfully." She sighed in relief.

"Now let's get you inside where you can get warm."

"I'm warm enough," Lexie countered, but she didn't stop Simon from wrapping an arm around her back and rushing her to the front door.

By the time they got inside, she was hot and not from the room's temperature. Pulling away from him, she dropped the blanket and took off her wet jacket, which he took from her.

Kicking off her equally wet boots and socks and dropping them by the door, she said, "I'm heading straight for the shower."

"Good idea."

She thought he meant good idea *for her* until a few minutes later. As she stood in the shower, just letting the hot water pound her, a nude Simon opened the glass door and slipped inside.

"Simon…"

This wasn't part of the deal. He'd agreed to sleep on the couch. So why couldn't she make herself remind him of that promise?

"I just want to check you for injuries," he said, "since you were too stubborn to go to an E.R. or clinic."

The way he was inspecting her body made Lexie's toes curl, and something warm and fluid unfurled inside her. She didn't want to be alone. She wanted safe arms around her and assurances that everything was going to be all right.

He was thoroughly wet now, and the water made his skin gleam and accentuated the incredible sculpted musculature of the body she'd once known nearly as well as her own.

"What makes you an expert?" she asked, meaning to tease him.

"Field experience."

He was serious.

She felt heartsick for him.

What Simon must have endured for more than a decade was something she couldn't fathom. Having to play doctor for his comrades out of necessity seemed unreal to her. By comparison, her life with all its daily dramas had been a picnic. She'd always had her family to love and support her. And she'd had their daughter.

While Simon had been caught in a living hell.

Now under the water with her, he turned her around, checked her body gently but thoroughly for any injury. The more he touched her, the less likely Lexie thought it would be that he would spend the night on the couch.

Why should she push him away from her when being with him was what she wanted? What she needed. What *he* needed.

The danger they'd shared had bonded them in a way she didn't quite understand. Even while part of her was frightened of what Simon might have become, there was a stronger-than-ever attraction to him. That scary part of him had protected her, she reminded herself, would keep her and their daughter safe until they found the answers that would bring down the perpetrators of the horrendous human trafficking operation.

He turned her again, ran his hands over her ribs.

Suddenly consumed by physical hunger, she couldn't meet his eyes, but looked down and realized that examining her had exactly the same effect on him. Thrown back into the past, she remembered the things they'd done for months until finally giving in to their passions and sleeping together that one magic night.

Before she could stop herself, she was touching him…lowering herself to her knees…kissing him…tasting him. Water drummed against her back as she took his soft tip into her mouth, loving the salty taste of him.

He groaned and threaded his fingers in her hair, and held her head tight up against him.

At seventeen, she'd become very practiced at this with him, but now at thirty, she felt like an amateur, wasn't sure if she was taking him deep enough or sucking hard enough or using her tongue cleverly enough to please him.

"Oh, Lexie, baby," he growled, pulling her up and lifting her off her feet.

The next thing she knew, her back was against the wet, slippery tile and her legs were wrapping around his hips and he was homing in on her like they'd done this on a regular basis for the last thirteen years. She was already drenched inside and he slipped in easily. Opening wider, she urged him in deeper until she had all of him.

"This is where I want to be," he murmured in her ear.

"This is where I feel safe," she admitted softly, trying to erase the memory of what had happened, of the fear she'd tasted, barely an hour before. She touched the scar on his chest, wondered if Simon ever really felt safe anymore.

They held each other, shower water raining down on them, and didn't move until the anticipation built and built. Finally he withdrew a little and pushed back inside. Her back was pressed against the wall, and he let go of her, found her breasts, tweaked her nipples the way she remembered he used to do.

"Touch yourself," he whispered in her ear, leaning back to give her access.

Her breath caught in her throat as she slid a hand between them. While they'd only slept together that once, they'd tried just about everything else before-hand. He'd loved it when she would touch and stroke herself and let him watch.

He was watching her now, his features tense with his desire. Sensation swirled through her, growing more urgent with each stroke.

"Rub harder," he whispered, and make his

strokes last longer. "I want you to come with me. I'll try to hold on."

Then he leaned over and kissed her openmouthed, and it didn't take her long to reach the frenzy he sought. Pressing his hands against the wall on either side of her head, he rocked into her faster and harder so their rhythms matched, until, at last, they reached the pinnacle, crying out, kissing each other like it might be the last time.

Which indeed it might, Lexie realized, wrapping her arms around his neck and holding on tight as if she would never let him go.

Zanko or another gun for hire could get to them.

Or Simon could simply realize he'd made a mistake in coming back to Jenkins Cove and take off for parts unknown.

This might be the last night she would have with the man she loved—a reason to make it memorable enough to last her for a lifetime.

LEXIE ARRIVED at Drake House the next morning in the garden center's delivery truck. Phil Cardon was driving. She wondered if he'd noticed that they were being followed.

She glanced back just once to see Simon's truck ease by the gate. He'd insisted on following her, had made her promise that before she left Drake House, she would call him on his cell so that he could come back to do the same.

Having spent the night in his arms, she had soft feelings for Simon. A yearning that wouldn't go away. She wanted to believe that he would stay for her. For their daughter. Give her a real family of her own. But another part of her thought that would be highly unlikely, especially in light of the Simon she'd seen in that abandoned boatyard.

Phil parked the truck and they got out, then began unloading the greenery from the back.

"Hey, did you ever find the owner of that key you showed me the other day?" Phil asked as they hauled out a couple of small balsams for the upstairs parlors.

The mention of the key jerked Lexie to attention. "No. Why?"

"Just wondering. So what did you do with it?"

Pulse thudding, she kept her voice even as she lied. "I threw it away."

"But it belonged to someone. You didn't turn it in to Chief Hammer?"

"It was only a key."

"Still. The owner's probably pretty peeved he lost it."

She'd bet he was. *But what was Phil's interest in something so seemingly minor?* she wondered as they each carried a tree into the foyer and up the stairs. She couldn't believe he hadn't forgotten about the key the moment he'd said it wasn't his and he'd never seen it.

Unless *he'd* been lying...

Could something other than curiosity underlie his interest? Had he told someone about the key? The owner who'd then come after her twice? Or had her assailant been Phil himself?

Phil had never had a regular job since moving to Jenkins Cove several years ago. He'd taken odd jobs, worked for her during the holidays and on big landscaping jobs. And yet he lived in a decent house, never actually appeared to hurt for cash.

Because he had a secret job that paid him well?

Human trafficking?

Were all his side jobs just a cover?

Lexie shook herself as the reached the parlors. What was she doing, trying to pin something so awful on Phil just because he had asked about the key?

Apparently the conversation with Simon the night before had set her up to be suspicious of everyone. Who would she think was guilty next?

Needing some respite from the trauma of the attack in the boatyard—a trauma eased but not erased by a night spent in Simon's arms—Lexie determined to put the human trafficking operation out of mind, at least while she was working at Drake House.

AFTER MAKING SURE that Lexie was safe at Drake House, Simon decided to do some investigating on his own. He drove back out to the mass grave. No patrol car idled there—Lexie had told him that she'd heard Chief Hammer had stopped trying to cover the area, not only because he was short-handed, but because no one wanted to go near the place. Even so, Simon made sure to hide the truck, just in case a patrol car drove by.

Stopping in front of the swampy area, he paused and looked around, wondering if the ghost of the dead kid made daylight appearances. There was mood lighting, courtesy of a sky that had grown gray with the threat of rain or snow, but there was no fog, no ghost. A wry smile played on Simon's lips as he moved on, around the area in a direction he hadn't yet taken.

There was a road down to the pier and warehouse where the surgeries had been performed, but not knowing if anyone might be wandering around down there, a cautious Simon had determined to go on foot, to stay within the treeline, to remain a ghost.

Lexie had told him the warehouse was probably a half mile or more off the main road, but that was an easy five minutes or so for a man as fit as he was. The sun had melted off the snow most places, but the woods were protected, and patches remained here and there. From what he remembered, snow never lasted that long here. Not cold enough.

As Simon jogged down a path through the trees, he thought about the night before, about the promise of a different life—one filled with more nights like that. With happiness. With that family he'd always wanted. What would Katie think if she suddenly learned that she had a father she hadn't known was alive? Would she recognize him from the market? Be freaked out? Or be happy that he existed?

Katie wouldn't be happy if she knew about his past, not any more than Lexie was. Not that she had said so. But she'd overheard his threats against Zanko and had seen him in action. That gave her some idea of what he was. While she'd made love to him, had held him as if she would never let him go, he was certain that in the end she would do so, if not for her own sake, for their daughter's.

Katie was Lexie's number one concern…just as it should be.

And as it should be for him. Both mother and daughter were his concern, and as such, they would be better off if he left after he made sure that justice was done.

Not wanting personal thoughts to distract him as he neared his destination, Simon turned off that part of his mind and tuned up his senses. A moment later, he heard voices, though he couldn't make out what they were saying, since the forest muffled any sound.

Slowing, Simon moved to the tree line where he could better see the road leading to the warehouse, which was practically within spitting distance. The decrepit old building was made of weathered wood, with boards missing on both sides. It hung partly over the water as if growing from the cattails that lined the shore. He could see yellow crime scene tape flapping in the wind.

Closer to him, two men stood out on the pier, one decked out in a wetsuit, hood, gloves, boots and full face mask, an air tank strapped across his back.

What the hell? Did he really mean to go into the water at this time of year? For what purpose?

The man jumped off the pier backwards, while the second guy watched. With close-cropped, sandy-brown hair and a weather-beaten, jowly face set in a scowl, the man on the pier looked familiar to Simon. He was dressed like a workman in jeans, heavy boots and a canvas jacket. It took Simon a while to identify the guy, but suddenly his memory kicked in.

Doug Heller. Cliff Drake's right-hand man and one of their prime suspects.

What the hell was *he* up to?

Simon wanted to go out there and *make* the man talk, but he held himself in check. He had to remain a ghost for a little while longer.

But a little while stretched into minutes, then into nearly half an hour. The water couldn't be very deep here along the shore, so the tank would last quite a while. Heller edged up and down the pier, apparently watching the diver's movements. The sky was getting darker and wisps of fog were rolling in over the water. Heller couldn't hide his impatience and began stomping around the pier, once taking a cell call, his voice too low for Simon to hear his conversation.

Finally, a dark shape broke the water's surface. Heller threw the other man a rope and hauled him up out of the water and onto the boards. His back was to Simon as he removed his gloves, mask and hood. He was empty-handed, which seemed to drive Heller into a fury.

"What do you mean you didn't find it?"

Simon tuned in, barely caught the shouted words.

"…telling you…wasn't there."

"…has to be."

"Then you go…find…"

"…through with…"

Simon caught enough to get the drift of the argument.

The man stomped toward the warehouse and only when Heller yelled, "Wait a minute!" did he turn back.

Simon immediately recognized the puffy, beard-stubbled face.

Hans Zanko!

There it was, proof of collusion between the man who'd tried to kill Lexie and him the night before and Doug Heller, one of their suspects.

Simon quickly took out his cell phone and snapped a couple of photos of the two as Heller caught up to Zanko and spoke in a tone too low for Simon to hear.

Both men disappeared into the warehouse, leaving Simon playing twenty questions with himself about what the hell they'd been up to.

He knew he had to find out.

He settled down, his back against a tree trunk, to wait and to think things through.

All along, Lexie had maintained that Heller had to be the guilty one. Apparently, she'd been correct.

But how to prove it to the satisfaction of the authorities?

Maybe whatever Heller had expected Zanko to find in that water would provide a clue…

Chapter Twelve

After the men drove off, Simon waited awhile, then cautiously approached the warehouse. Dismantling the lock only took a minute. Still careful, Simon entered and focused his senses. No one else here. Closing the door behind him just in case some cop on patrol came along, he waited for his eyes to adjust to the dark before moving around inside. The only shafts of light came through the high windows.

The foundation was cement, weeds growing through cracks here and there. The place looked empty but for a padded table that might belong in an operating room. The place was drafty, with odd cold spots that sent a chill up Simon's back.

How did he know it wasn't haunted by the people detained there who hadn't made it out?

Hardening himself against the sheer inhumanity that had gone on in this place, Simon looked around until he spotted a sheltered area in one corner and headed for it, only to find the wetsuit hanging on a pipe over a drain. The rest of the gear had been laid out on a table. He checked the tank. About twelve minutes of air left.

It would have to do.

Simon wasn't looking forward to getting into near-freezing water, but he'd been trained to deal with any conditions, and he'd been trained to scuba dive—he'd even done so on a couple of missions. Searching for some lost object in shallow waters would be easy by comparison.

Quickly, he donned the Thinsulate underwear that went under the wetsuit, then the suit itself. Zanko was a stockier man than he and, as Simon had expected, the neck seal especially was a tad loose. Nothing he could do about that, he thought as he pulled on the boots and then the hood, except pray that the gap wouldn't let too much cold water inside the suit or he would be vulnerable to hypothermia. He added weights and a buoyancy compensator and the tank, then grabbed the face mask, regulator and underwater light and left the warehouse for the pier.

Where to go in?

Heller had been a pretty accurate marker as to where Zanko had searched. He hadn't quite gone to the end of the pier, so that's where Simon chose to begin. Undoubtedly, they'd been looking for an item someone had dropped. Now if only he had a clue as to what that might be…

Simon secured the face mask, checked over the rest of his equipment, then jumped into the water, which was only about twelve feet deep here. Even so, a trickle of icy water oozed its way in through his loose neck seal.

Starting at the very tip of the pier, Simon turned on the underwater light and inspected every square foot. The only things that immediately caught his eye were plastic beer can holders and pages of a newspaper that hadn't yet dissolved. As he went on, he found more garbage dropped by careless humans. Certainly nothing of value.

The bay's water continued to trickle down inside his wetsuit. His discomfort growing, Simon checked his air supply time.

Five minutes left.

As he inched along the pier back toward the shore, he thought fast. If Heller had believed the lost object was still here somewhere, then Simon figured it was something with weight. And if the object had dropped from the pier, it should still be around. Tides moved things, even heavy things. But an object with weight shouldn't have gone far.

Four minutes…

Though he kept checking at every piling, turned over anything that stuck out of the bay's bottom,

Simon was getting closer and closer to the area near the shore where Zanko had spent the most time searching.

But Zanko hadn't searched where the warehouse hung over the shoreline.

Three minutes...

Simon tried to ignore the blossoming cold inside his wetsuit as he finished checking the length of the pier. That brought him into shallower water, where he turned his underwater light along the shoreline. Part of the warehouse hung over the water's edge that was lined with cattails. All kinds of things were caught in the stalks, which grew to more than six feet.

Two minutes...

Clenching his jaw so his teeth wouldn't chatter, he moved under the edge of the warehouse and searched and pulled at things woven into the shoreline vegetation. Frustration ate at him as he struck out again.

One minute...

And then he spotted something big and shiny near the edge of the warehouse, close to where the road above ended. He raced to the spot.

Zero minutes.

Simon surfaced and gasped, tried to shake off the chill now affecting his efficiency. Tempering his breath, he took a deep one and dived. He got a gloved hand on the object that was long and heavy, but the cattails seemed to have grown around it, clutching it. He started ripping at the vegetation, but before he could free the object he had to come up for more air.

Down he went a second time and nearly managed to pull the object free.

A third dive and he succeeded, taking possession of a metal object shaped like a long cup.

Surfacing with no air to spare, Simon took a moment and simply breathed. Tendrils of fog snaked along the water and up over the shoreline. The outside air had changed, hitting him in gusts. About to climb out onto shore, he stopped when he heard a vehicle moving toward him. Grasping the trophy to his chest, he threw himself back into the cattails close to the warehouse and listened, ready to sink below water level if necessary.

The vehicle crept closer and Simon's pulse thundered, the extra adrenaline warming him. Had Heller and Zanko returned to renew their search for the trophy? Or had someone else come out here to look for it?

Simon waited chin-deep in the water for what felt like forever, but was actually only a few minutes. The vehicle never stopped, merely circled and moved away. Simon moved, too, so he could get a look at the vehicle that turned out to be a Jenkins Cove patrol car. Apparently, the local cops were still on the job, after all.

Heaving a sigh of relief that he hadn't been dis-
covered, Simon lifted the trophy to see exactly what
the hell he'd found. Inscribed on the base of the cup
was the name of the race—UK Challenge Cup—
and the name of the winner.

Clifford Drake.

"WHAT ARE YOU DOING HERE?" Lexie asked when her
mother walked into the ballroom with Katie in tow.

"Nice to see you, too, sweetheart."

Lexie hugged her mother, who was several inches
shorter with a soft, round body. Her glasses were
pushed up into her dark hair threaded with gray, and
she wore a smear of flour on one cheek.

"It *is* nice to see you. Just a surprise." One Lexie
didn't appreciate at this moment, considering the
circumstances. Besides, she was just about to call
Simon again. He hadn't picked up the last two times
she'd tried to get him and she was worried. She
hugged her daughter and reminded herself that at
least Katie's bodyguard had their back. "Hey, kiddo,
how's the cookie-making?"

"This morning, Nana showed me how to make six
kinds of cookies from one dough recipe."

"Well, good. I expect you'll keep us well-stocked
with goodies from now on." She looked back to her
mother. "So what's going on?"

"We decided to take a break from baking. Katie

wanted to stop at home so she could get her iPod and some fresh clothes. And then she insisted that we come here so she could get a sneak peak at what you've done with the place. I was curious myself. You've outdone yourself, Lexie. It never looked this good when Jonathan was alive and your dad and I did the decorating."

Lexie gave her mother another hug. "You exaggerate, but thanks."

"This looks really rad, Mom." Katie twirled and dipped in the center of the ballroom as if she were dancing with an invisible partner. "Next year you've got to hire me to help."

Lexie started. "You're asking me for a job?" Her daughter was growing up way too fast. "Aren't you a little young to be worrying about working?"

"I *will* be a teenager by then," Katie reminded her, her snub nose in the air. "Teenagers have needs that allowances just don't cover."

"Okay," Lexie said, holding herself back from laughing, "I'll keep that in mind."

She spent the next ten minutes showing her mother and daughter every public room so they could see everything. She even had one of the lighting guys turn on the snow effect.

But all the while she had to hold her anxiety in check. What was Simon up to? Had he gotten into the warehouse?

When Mom and Katie left with hugs and kisses all around, Lexie pulled out her cell and tried again.

No answer.

A chill settled in her middle and she was suddenly afraid that Simon had gotten more than he'd bargained for.

What in the world was going on?

THOUGH SIMON DIDN'T KNOW the significance of the trophy being in the water, he was certain it was what Heller had sent Zanko down to find. Thinking it wouldn't do to mess with any prints on the metal, just in case they would prove to be significant, he kept the diving gloves on until he got back into the warehouse and shoved the trophy into a ditty bag that had been left with the diving gear.

Then he stripped, dried himself off as best he could, and dressed in his blissfully warm clothes. Even so, he was cold to the core and trying not to shake inside. A jog back to the truck should warm him.

Not wanting anyone to figure out what he'd been up to, he put everything back the way he'd found it. Hopefully, the damp undergarments he left folded on the table wouldn't give him away.

Then, after making sure he was still alone, Simon left the warehouse, resetting the door lock, after which he made for the tree line, ditty bag in hand.

What the hell should he do with the trophy until

they figured out what part it had played in things? he wondered. Too risky to leave it in the back of his truck or to store it in Lexie's house. Better if he hid it someplace in the open. Someplace where no one would think to look. Like somewhere in the swamp.

Thinking he'd find a good spot in the area where he'd parked, he started for his truck.

The wind had picked up, as had the cold. Rather, cold spots. They followed him into the woods. Gusts brought with them fine sprays of snow, though he hadn't thought it was supposed to snow until later. A shiver raced through Simon and he tried to blame it on his time in the water. But there was something different about the way this felt, as if the air pressure itself had changed. Similar to the way he'd felt the other night. He stopped and peered into the gloom between two trees where he focused on waves of energy that stretched and whirled and morphed into a figure that appeared to be human.

The ghost had returned.

"What do you want me to see this time?" Simon whispered, the cold suddenly taking him in its grip.

He felt an urgency, a force even, pushing him toward the faint apparition that seemed to be taking on substance. The kid appeared in his thin leather coat, the mop of pale hair falling into his face. His dark eyes were sorrowful, his mouth an angry slash in the too-pale face.

"What is it?"

The kid seemed agitated as he waved for Simon to follow, then whirled and pressed deeper into the woods, and Simon couldn't have stopped himself from following the spirit if he'd wanted to. It was as if invisible strings were tugging at him, connecting him to the dead kid, making him subject to the will of someone who didn't even exist on this plane.

Instead, he followed a swirl of mist that, to him, seemed to be full of fury.

Why? Simon wondered.

Suddenly the kid stopped, twisted around to face Simon as if trying to tell him something. Or show him something. The apparition was losing substance by the second.

Simon jogged across the short expanse, but the closer he got, the fainter the wraith became. It hovered for a moment, then seemed to dissolve into the blowing snow sweeping through the woods.

"What the hell?"

Simon stopped short. Why had the ghost appeared to him again, only to disappear before there was anything to see? Or was something there and he just had to look more closely?

He stepped forward, putting one foot in front of the other like a robot, unable to stop himself until he was within a yard of where the ghost had disappeared. What now? He turned, examining the trees around him as the fog mysteriously rolled back on all sides, as if framing the suspect area.

Nothing!

What the hell?

About to give up and go back to the truck, Simon felt the earth beneath his foot give a little. He looked down. The ground where he stood had been newly turned. No traces of pine needles or leaves covered it. None of the snow that limned the ground around it, delineating the small area.

Had something been buried here?

Wishing he had a shovel, Simon started pushing at some of the soft dirt with his foot. It scooped away easily. A strange feeling shot through him as he gauged the length and width of the patch of nude earth. Hesitating only a second, he put the ditty bag down, got to his knees and started scooping with his hands. Within seconds he uncovered part of what was buried there.

A man, the side of his head bashed in and bloody, stared up at him through lifeless eyes.

Simon hadn't officially met the man, but he recognized him. Ned Perry, the land developer so desperate to get his hands on shoreline land, even one with a mass grave. The man he'd overheard trying to blackmail Brandon Drake.

His heart thundered as he inspected the wound as best he could without touching the guy. He'd seen fatal wounds like that before—rubble falling on his comrades, cracking open their heads like fragile eggs.

But this wound hadn't been caused by rubble, but by a directed strike—he was certain of it. It looked like someone had taken a baseball bat to Perry's head.

Or a big metal trophy...

Simon swore. Had he really been dragging around the murder weapon?

Opening the ditty bag, he stared at the cup without touching it. No blood, of course, not after being in the water. He didn't even know if prints would hold up.

He had a body and undoubtedly the murder weapon.

What now?

Could he trust the local cops to get it right?

Figuring Perry's death somehow had to do with the human trafficking situation, Simon first called Bray and gave him the scoop, asked him to call that state detective brother-in-law of his and get him down here fast.

"Just don't mention my name," Simon added before hanging up.

He wiped the ditty bag to get rid of his own fingerprints, then dumped the trophy a short distance from the body—near enough to be found, far enough away not to be obvious—then jogged to the truck. Only when he was in it and on the road away from the site and heading toward Drake House did he call the Jenkins Cove Police and ask for the chief.

"Hammer here," came a drawl on the other end.

"I'd like to report a murder."

"Who is this?"

"Someone who doesn't want to get involved." Simon wasn't about to identify himself—not yet, not before they got more answers.

"Is this some kind of a joke?" Hammer demanded. "Who put you up to this?"

"I was taking a walk through the woods and nearly stumbled over the body. It's near the mass grave."

"Another one of them." Hammer sounded bored.

"No, this one's fresh. The victim is Ned Perry. You'd better get down here, Hammer, if you want to keep your job. The state police have already been informed, and Detective Rand McClellan is already on his way."

Chapter Thirteen

"Why are we leaving now?" Phil asked, when Lexie insisted they stop for the day. "We still need to finish the last couple strings of outside lights."

"The sun is already down. It'll be dark soon," she said by way of a plausible excuse. "They can wait until tomorrow morning. I've already told Marie we're heading out."

Lexie chose to leave it at that, not embellish. The fancier the story, the more likely it would raise suspicions.

Phil shrugged and got behind the wheel of the truck and pulled down the drive. Though she looked for Simon's truck near the gate, Lexie didn't see it until they were on the road and she caught a glimpse of it in the sideview mirror.

His call had at first relieved her—she'd begun to fear the worst, that something terrible had happened to him—then had made her tense. Ned Perry dead. He'd been obnoxious, but that wasn't enough reason for someone to want to murder him. What had he been up to?

The plan was to go back to the shop, get her SUV and then rendezvous with Simon at her place.

But as they headed for town, two local police cars and one unmarked police car, all with lights flashing, were cutting onto a gravel road that led into the woods not far from the mass gravesite.

"Hey, something's up. Let's see what's going on," Phil said, following before she could stop him.

She threw an apprehensive look over her shoulder. This wasn't part of the plan. What would Simon do?

He kept going on the main road.

Now she was really anxious. Why in the heck had Phil done that?

Suddenly she realized that the police cars ahead had been abandoned, along with several other state vehicles and an ambulance. Uniformed and plain-clothes officers were on foot, gathering around a spot a hundred yards away.

Phil pulled over. "Something big must be going on. Let's go see."

Again, before she could object, he acted. He flew out of the truck and jogged through the trees. What did he think he was doing? The police weren't going to let him anywhere near the crime scene.

Lexie stayed behind and used her cell to call Simon. When he answered, she asked, "Where are you?"

"Down the road on the other side of the grave. What happened?"

"Phil took things in his own hands. Literally."

"Get in as close as they let you, see what you can overhear. I'll be around, but out of sight."

Wishing they could be together, that she could feel Simon's supportive arm around her, Lexie approached the knot of officials, but didn't want to get too close, even if they let her. She didn't want to see Ned Perry with his head bashed in.

Chief Hammer was consulting with the state detective, Rand McClellan, whom Lexie had seen before but not met. A crime scene investigator, a couple of EMTs, and a few reporters were on the spot, too. She figured it wouldn't be long before a television news crew showed up.

Phil Cardon was nowhere to be found, making her wonder where he'd disappeared to, why he'd been so hell-bent on following the police cars to a crime scene, only to disappear.

Still looking for him, Lexie hung back, not wanting anyone to notice her and make a big deal about her being where she didn't belong.

"Looks like he was murdered sometime last night," came a deep male voice from the knot of people. "Struck with an unusually shaped object... could be something round."

"Start looking for anything that might be the weapon," McClellan told the uniformed officers.

Lexie backed off, circled the investigation team and quietly wandered off in the direction Simon might be hiding. The woods were gloomy. It would soon be dark. She wished things didn't have to be like this, that Simon could be out in the open, that she could be seen with him rather than sneaking around to find him.

A "psst" got her attention and she looked to her right.

Standing in the shelter of a tree, Simon indicated they should move farther into the woods, away from the activity. She quickly complied and they backed off another dozen yards.

"So what did you hear?" he asked, keeping his voice low.

"Only that Perry was probably killed last night. The question is why."

"Considering how I found him, I would guess it has something to do with the human trafficking operation."

"How *did* you find him?"

"It was the kid again, the one I saw murdered. He led me right to the grave."

The ghost again. Simon was a rational man. Marie and Chelsea were both rational, too, and yet they'd both had experiences with the afterlife. And what about Bray? His touching the key had led them to Anna Bencek. If Simon thought he saw a ghost, Lexie believed it.

"But Ned Perry?" she murmured. "I mean if he *was* involved in the trafficking, he should have been well-off. He was so desperate to make money he was even willing to buy land that had been a mass grave."

"I didn't say he was directly involved. But he could have found out something. Maybe something about that land. What if he was blackmailing the wrong person?"

"You mean Brandon," Lexie said, remembering the conversation between the two men that Simon had overheard. "I don't believe that, either."

"You don't want to believe it. And you're probably correct," he conceded.

Simon told her about his morning's activities, about Doug Heller's connection to Hans Zanko, about finding Cliff's racing trophy, which the men obviously had been searching for.

"Zanko tried to kill us, and he was looking for the trophy that was undoubtedly the murder weapon used on Perry. And right after I found it, the ghost led me to his body. It all has to be connected."

"The trophy...I heard them say Ned was struck by a round object."

"I dumped it in the area for them to find. Are you familiar with it?"

"I've seen it. Cliff kept it on *Drake's Passage,*"

she admitted, then hastily added, "which doesn't mean Cliff did it."

Simon nodded. "It's looking like Heller is our man. Now we just have to prove it, get our hands on those files before he decides to destroy the evidence. His prints are probably all over them."

"We just have to find the cabinet the key unlocks," Lexie said. "Which means we have to get into Drake Enterprises." Though she was reluctant to leave him, Lexie said, "I'd better get back, before Phil comes looking for me."

Simon whipped her against him for a quick kiss that left Lexie breathless.

"I'll be watching you," he promised.

Reminded of the way he'd been watching her the night before, Lexie flushed as she made her way back to the crime scene. Simon was becoming more and more real to her, and she was less and less willing to give him up. What could she do to keep him? To satisfy the part of him that had changed? To keep him from carrying the justice thing too far?

Halfway to the crime scene, she noticed a furtive movement ahead in the descending dark and slipped into the shadow of a large tree to see what was going on.

Phil Cardon was skulking away from the crime scene, something bulky under his jacket. About to confront him, she stopped when she realized he was being followed.

"Cardon, what do you think you're doing there?" Chief Hammer caught up to the man, grabbed him by the shoulder and spun him around. "Let me see what you're hiding."

Hammer didn't wait for Phil to cooperate, but opened Phil's jacket and pulled a large bag free from where the other man held it to his chest.

"Hey, you can't do that!" Phil said.

"I just did." Hammer opened the bag. He reached inside and hauled out the trophy. Then a look of comprehension colored his expression. "What the hell are you doing with this?"

"Hey, I found it. I figured it was worth something at a pawnshop. You can't blame a guy for trying to make a few extra bucks where he can, especially during the holidays."

Hammer grabbed Phil's arm and whirled him back toward the crime scene, saying, "We need to have a little chat."

Lexie stepped into a clearing and watched Phil try to squirm his way out of going with Hammer. The police chief had him in a tight hold and didn't seem about to let go.

What had Phil been doing with the trophy, undoubtedly the murder weapon? Why had he been trying to remove it from the scene of the crime?

By the time she got back to the crime scene, Ned's body was bagged and being carried to the ambulance. One of the officers was pushing Phil into a squad car. No doubt they were taking him in for questioning.

Did he have something to do with the murder? With the human trafficking?

Lexie didn't know what to think, but everything was coming to a head. They needed to find those files.

Before she could slip away, a man stepped in front of her. She stared at the finely cut overcoat for a few seconds before lifting her gaze to that of Detective Rand McClellan.

"What are you doing here?" he asked.

"I was hijacked," she said, her stomach doing a fast twirl. Thinking Bray Sloane had told his brother-in-law about Simon and her, she was tempted for a moment to confide in the state lawman. She wanted nothing more than for the state authorities to take over the investigation. "One of my seasonal workers was driving the truck. We were on our way back to the garden center when he saw the squads and decided to follow them."

"So where is this guy?"

"Chief Hammer has him."

A look of understanding crossed his face. "Ah."

"I'm Lexie Thornton," she said. When he didn't

react, she realized Bray hadn't said anything to him. And she knew she couldn't, either. If she did, she would betray Simon. Disappointed, she asked, "Can I go now?"

McClellan nodded. "Sure."

Getting into the truck, Lexie sped away from the crime scene as fast as she dared. Once on the main road, she headed for town and looked for Simon, but he didn't seem to be following, probably because some of the police cars were heading out, as well.

She called him. "I'm heading for the garden center to pick up my SUV."

"I'll meet you at your place. Don't go inside until I get there to go in with you."

"You'll be there ahead of me. I'm going to pick up dinner."

"Lexie—"

"Unless you want peanut butter and jelly sandwiches."

"Don't take any chances."

Lexie called in to a local café and ordered a couple of the blue plate specials—meat loaf, mashed potatoes and green beans—so they'd be ready by the time she got there.

Thornton Garden Center was already closed for the night and Carole was gone. Lexie traded the truck for her SUV and headed for home.

Waiting for her, Simon led the way inside, checking to make sure there hadn't been a break-in, before they sat down to eat at the kitchen table.

Lexie told him about Phil Cardon.

"He could be an accomplice," Simon said, "trying to get rid of evidence."

"Something I was wondering myself," Lexie said. She even wondered if Phil could have attacked her, but fearing Simon's reaction, she didn't voice the question. "If he's not arrested, I'm not sure I want him working for me."

"Does he have to work for you? Legally, I mean?"

"He's seasonal. I guess after we finish Drake House tomorrow morning, I can let him go. But what if his story about wanting to hock the trophy is true?"

"You are too trusting."

At least he didn't say naive.

"Drake Enterprises is officially locked up until Monday morning," Lexie said. "So how do we get in?"

"Leave that to me. No problem."

Another reminder of Simon's past. The mouthful of food nearly stuck in Lexie's throat and she washed it down with half a glass of water. Would Simon ever be satisfied living a normal life again? She couldn't imagine it.

"So we're going to check out Drake Enterprises tonight?" she asked.

"That's the plan."

A thrill shot through Lexie as she realized they might find their answer tonight. Then what?

"If we find the files, will that be enough proof for the authorities?"

"I don't know. It'll be enough for me."

Lexie wanted to ask what he meant by that, but she was afraid she might not want to hear the answer.

They finished eating in silence, after which Simon said, "I'll clear."

"I'll get the key."

Even as she left the kitchen, Lexie had some doubts about what they were doing. This kind of a search should be left to the authorities. Then again, she doubted that Chief Hammer believed in ghosts or in psychic abilities like the one that allowed Bray to see the names on the files.

Even if they found the files, how were they going to explain everything?

Maybe she never should have kept the key. But a lost key wasn't exactly something the police would want to be bothered with. Scary how everything had escalated so quickly.

Lifting the finial off the newel, Lexie looked inside and gasped.

The key was gone.

Chapter Fourteen

"Whoever got in and took the key is really good," Simon said. "I didn't see any sign of a break-in."

Suddenly it hit Lexie. "Katie! Mom brought her by the house to pick up some clothes earlier. She must have found it."

Lexie hurried to the phone and called her parents' number. Her mother answered.

"Mom, I need to speak to Katie."

"She's up in her room. She said she was tired and wanted to go to bed early."

Was she getting sick? Katie never wanted to go to bed early. "Can you get her, please?"

Lexie covered the mouthpiece and met Simon's gaze. "Why would she have taken the key?"

"Maybe she looked to see if you left a note…and thought the key was for her."

"That makes sense," Lexie agreed. "We'll have to stop at the house to get it from her."

Her mother came back on the phone. "Honey, I

don't know how to tell you this but…Katie's not there. I—I think she left the house."

"What?" Panic gripped Lexie—had someone kidnapped her daughter? She looked to Simon. "Where would she go—and at night?"

Simon immediately flipped open his cell and walked to the other end of the room, undoubtedly to check with the man who was supposed to be guarding their daughter.

Then her mother said, "That party you wouldn't let her go to…it's tonight. Maybe she went despite your telling her she couldn't go."

That had to be it, Lexie thought. Better that than where her mind had started to take her. "What was the name of that boy?"

"Josh Pearson. He lives a couple blocks east of me. I'll go there right now."

"No, I'm her mother." Lexie grabbed a pad of paper and pen. "Where does he live?" She made note of the address and hung up at the same time Simon closed his cell and cursed under his breath.

"He didn't see a thing."

"I don't understand how she slipped by him, unless he was asleep," said Lexie, annoyance, anger and fear suffusing her voice.

"She must have gone out the back door. He simply couldn't be in two places at once."

Lexie nodded and headed for the door. "We're going to a party."

They threw on their jackets and left the house. Lexie went directly to the SUV and Simon climbed into the passenger seat. Lexie's stomach clenched at the thought that Simon and Katie would meet face-to-face.

"What are you doing?" she demanded.

"Making sure my kid is okay. You can introduce me as your date."

"She'll know that's a lie." The moment the words were out of her mouth, Lexie flushed. Simon didn't have to know she didn't date, but it was too late to take it back.

"You can tell her there's a first time for everything," he said as she started the engine.

Truth be told, despite her doubts about putting father and daughter together before they'd worked anything out, before she'd had time to prepare Katie, Lexie was glad Simon was with her. She could use his strength, and his sense of calm was catching.

Ten minutes later, she double-parked outside a house that was obviously the scene of a party. All the lights were on and music and shouts drifted out to the street.

Turning on her flashers, Lexie said, "Wait for me here," and jumped out of the vehicle.

As she ran up the steps, she looked through the

front bay windows, but didn't see Katie. A knot formed in her stomach. Katie had to be there. She *had* to be.

A sign on the door said to COME ON IN—IT'S OPEN, so she did. Heart pounding, she looked around at kids who were eating and talking in one room, dancing in the other. She recognized only a few of them. She didn't know many of the high school kids. When she didn't spot Katie right away, her pulse began to race.

What if they were wrong and Katie wasn't here, after all?

What if someone had gotten into the house and had taken her?

Just then she spotted a girl named Megan, an older friend of her daughter's.

"Megan, hi," she said, forcing a smile. "Have you seen Katie?"

"I think she's in the kitchen." Megan pointed her in the right direction.

Relieved, Lexie said, "Thanks," and moved through the crowd to the kitchen.

She spotted Katie immediately. Rather than being with the high school kids she'd wanted to be part of, Katie was with adults. Two women were getting food together and Katie was helping them by placing sandwiches they made on a tray. She had a big grin on her face and nodded at something one of the women said.

Lexie waited until her system righted and called, "Katie!"

Katie's head whipped around and her eyes went wide. "Mom?"

"Let's go."

A mulish expression settled on her daughter's face and she didn't budge. The two women looked distressed but didn't interfere.

"Katie, *now.*"

Suddenly Katie rushed across the kitchen, eyes bright, and sailed right past her. Lexie nodded to the women, who gave her sympathetic looks, then followed her daughter, who grabbed her jacket from a coat tree and stormed straight out of the house and down the front steps.

"Get in the backseat."

"What? Why?" Katie demanded.

"Because the front seats are occupied."

Katie did as she was told and slammed the door.

Lexie slid behind the wheel and gripped it for a moment. "I'm disappointed in you, Katie Thornton. You scared Nana to death. You scared me. You deliberately disobeyed me. What were you thinking?"

"That I didn't want to be an old stick-in-the-mud like you. I wanted to have some fun in my life. But it looks like you were doing that, too, behind my back."

"Don't speak to your mother that way," Simon said, his tone flat but firm. "You owe her your respect. She was very worried about you and with good reason."

Lexie thought Katie might argue with Simon, but the girl didn't say a word as they pulled away from the curb.

"I'm taking you back to your grandparents' house, Katie. I don't want to disappoint them because they were looking forward to spending time with you. But if I do, I want to know that you won't act without permission again."

Katie's voice was sulky as she asked, "You're not grounding me?"

"I didn't say that, but that can wait until you're back home. In the meantime, I want you to promise me you won't try to sneak off again."

"All right. I promise!"

"One other thing…do you have the key that I left in the newel post?"

"I thought you left it for me." Katie's voice rose defensively. "Like it was some kind of puzzle I was supposed to figure out."

"No, Katie. I just put it there for temporary safekeeping."

"Safekeeping? Why?"

"I just didn't want to lose it," Lexie hedged, holding out an open hand by her shoulder. "May I have it, please?" She felt the metal press into her palm and let her fingers curl around it. "Thank you."

"You're not mad about the key, too, are you?"

"No, honey, I'm not angry about the key."

When they arrived at her parents' house, Lexie walked Katie inside and assured her parents that everything was all right and that their granddaughter had promised not to scare them again. Katie couldn't look at her, wouldn't speak to her, not even when Lexie gave her a one-armed hug and kissed the top of her head. Silently apologizing for any scares she'd given her own parents, she kissed them, too, before leaving.

When she got back into the SUV, she just sat there for a moment, trying to regain her equilibrium.

"Everything okay?" Simon asked.

"Fine. Is Katie's bodyguard out here?"

"In the dark car across the street."

"Good. Then we can go."

As she started off for Drake Enterprises, Lexie couldn't help but worry. Katie had been asserting herself more lately, had even openly defied her, but she'd never gone behind Lexie's back before. Or attacked her personally.

Remembering how Simon had stepped in, how Katie had responded to him, she said, "You surprised me before. You sounded like a father."

"Maybe because I *am* a father and I want to be part of our daughter's life."

Lexie had nothing to say to that.

SIMON HADN'T MISSED the way Lexie avoided the *father* reference. Because she didn't believe him? Or because she didn't want him to be a father to Katie?

He also hadn't missed that she hadn't introduced him to their daughter. Then, again, what could she have said about him under the circumstances?

The whole situation had simply been awkward.

What he got from the incident, though, was to see firsthand a mother's love. Lexie was tough and focused, a lioness with her cub, even in the face of their daughter's temper. Katie had been a little snot to her, as kids could be when they didn't get their own way. Though he'd interrupted, he hadn't said what he'd longed to say—that Katie should appreciate what she had because she could lose it any time.

Just as he had.

Simon forced his mind away from the personal and concentrated on the task ahead.

"Have you ever been at Drake Enterprises at night?"

"Several times. We do their Christmas decorations. And then I went with Marie once. She was meeting Brandon there after a board meeting."

"What about security?"

"No one mans the security desk after hours," Lexie said, "but there is a guard that makes rounds every so often. Maybe once an hour."

"We should be able to avoid him." At least Simon hoped they could. He didn't want to have an altercation with some poor guy just doing his low-end job. "So you know the layout of the building."

"Somewhat."

"The executive offices?"

"They're on the second floor. I've only taken an elevator up, but there are at least two sets of stairs, as well."

"We'll take the stairs then." The elevator would create noise and bring the security guard running.

Just outside of town, Lexie pulled onto Yacht Basin Road, and when it split she took the right branch. Drake Enterprises was straight ahead, overlooking the water. She pulled the car over to the side of the drive under a stand of trees just before they reached the two-story brick building.

She said, "I figure the security guard won't be looking for anything back here."

"Good thinking."

And good that trees lined the road and provided them with cover all the way to the building.

Simon led the way, fine-tuning his senses to any noise or movement. The only thing he heard was the water washing against the shoreline. Nothing in sight moved.

"We'll get in through the loading dock door," he told Lexie. And prayed there would be nothing extraordinary about the locks that protected it.

A moment later they were on the dock, under the

shelter of a canopy. Noting the alarm system, Simon removed some tools from his pocket and disabled it. Then he started working on the door locks.

"Is all this something you learned to do in your former life?" Lexie asked, her uneven voice revealing her nerves.

"I had to learn to do a lot of things that I never thought I would do," Simon returned. Breaking and entering were among the least offensive of the skills he had been forced to learn. "When we get inside, we'll have no idea where the security guard is, so we'll need to be silent. Use sign language."

The lock clicked and he put a finger to his lips, then cracked the door and listened intently for several seconds before opening it fully and showing her inside. It was dark, but Lexie indicated that they needed to go down the long corridor to a set of double doors inset with small windows that glowed softly against the black corridor.

When they got to the windows, Simon looked through one to the lobby where a few fixtures were dimmed, allowing him enough light to view the whole space. A young man in a gray uniform trimmed with black stood by the front windows, looking out. Simon held a hand up to tell Lexie to wait. A moment later, the guard moved off, crossed the room and went through a door on the other side of the security desk.

Simon opened the door slowly, concentrating on

making no sound. He urged Lexie through and, with only the equivalent of an emergency light to guide them, she went straight for the stairs. Simon followed, then once in the stairwell moved past her.

At the top of the staircase, he stopped and listened, then cracked open the door to darkness. No light here. He looked to Lexie, who indicated that they should go to the left.

Simon nodded, took Lexie's hand and let her take the lead until a door slammed open down the hall. His pulse kicked up. The last thing he wanted was a confrontation. The young security guard was no Hans Zanko. Simon certainly didn't want to hurt him, which would surely happen if he didn't avoid the man, who must have come up that second set of stairs.

The dark down the corridor was suddenly broken by a strong beam of light that moved from side to side. Simon squeezed Lexie's hand to warn her, and immediately felt for the nearest doorway. He opened the door carefully so as not to make any noise, then pushed Lexie inside. He followed even as the corridor lights went on.

Simon felt another door just inside the first, opened that one and stepped inside, pulling Lexie with him. There was hardly room for both of them in what was a closet, hardly room to breathe. Coats and other clothing crushed against them, cocooning them together. Though the situation was tense, with Lexie's derriere pressed against him, Simon couldn't help but respond physically. When Lexie audibly caught her breath, he knew she noticed, and he suspected that she was equally turned on.

Fighting the distraction, he closed his eyes and listened intently as the sound of doors opening and closing echoed along the corridor. The security guard was doing more than a cursory job. He was taking careful inventory. Simon prayed he wasn't looking into every closet, too.

When he heard the office door open, Simon tensed, tightened his arm around Lexie. The guard was moving around…stopping…standing still for what felt like an interminable amount of time. Then he moved again and the office door closed behind him.

Simon didn't move. He listened to the security guard's progress as he made his way slowly down the corridor.

"What do we do?" Lexie whispered.

"Wait."

It was several minutes before the security guard strode back down the hall, stopping halfway. The mechanical groan and whir of the nearby elevator relieved Simon, who'd thought the man might have suspected they were there, hiding from him. He listened harder, made sure the doors swished open and closed and the elevator descended, before relaxing.

"Let's wait a minute longer to be sure," he whispered into Lexie's ear.

She nodded, her hair moving against his skin, and at that instant, Simon knew he'd never wanted her more. Not that he could have her, not here. Each minute he waited was torture, but each minute was necessary to keep from being found out.

Finally deciding that the guard was truly gone, that it was safe to leave the closet, he opened the door. They practically fell out together.

"That was close," Lexie whispered.

"Too close. Let's do this."

Leaving the office, Simon let Lexie lead him all the way to the end of the corridor. She stopped, felt around. Simon heard the sound of the doorknob being tested. Then the door swung inward and Lexie led him inside.

"This is the executive suite," she whispered in his ear.

Simon thought to tell her they could talk in low tones now, but the sensual vibes he was getting from her breath and sheer closeness stopped him from spoiling the moment.

"The receptionist sits out here. Cliff's office is to the right. Heller's office is to the left. Both overlook the water, of course."

"What about in between?" he whispered in return.

"The boardroom. Cliff's administrative assistant and Heller's secretary have offices outside the suite."

"Let's try Heller's office first." Holding her hand, he pulled her inside, closed the door and turned on a small desk lamp. "I think it's safe to talk now."

Lexie was examining the three file cabinets in Heller's office. "These are similar, but not identical." She tried to insert the key. "Nope. Doesn't even fit. I don't understand. We were so sure it was Heller."

Simon clenched his jaw. He'd been hoping to hit pay dirt, but apparently it was too much to expect on the first try.

"Cliff's office," Simon said, noting Lexie's dismayed expression before turning off the light.

But Cliff's cabinets were identical to those in Heller's office.

Lexie appeared relieved.

"There's still the boardroom," Simon said.

Lexie's relief seemed short-lived. "If it's in there, it could be either one of them."

Indeed, one end of the boardroom was an entire file and storage system. Both file drawer and door cabinets were decorated with the requisite leaf marquetry.

When he noticed Lexie staring at them as if she couldn't take a step forward, Simon asked, "You want me to try?"

She handed over the key.

Simon tried the first lock. The key slid in easily but didn't turn. He tried the second…third…all. The key opened none of them.

Frustration turned him rigid, made him want to beat on something. Someone.

A gentle hand on his arm startled him. He whipped around to face Lexie. "I don't get it," he said. "Can there be more of these cabinets in other offices?"

Lexie shrugged. "I wouldn't think so. I can't see just anyone having them."

Even so, they backtracked down the hall, checking office after office and finding nothing even close to a match.

They left the building the way they'd come and with as much care as they'd taken when they'd entered it. The only sign that they'd been there was the disabled alarm.

Not wanting anything to go wrong before they got out of the area, Simon left it unarmed, knowing it would warn the villain that his time of going undiscovered was drawing to an end.

LEXIE LOST HERSELF in the silence on the way home. Simon was driving. Just as well. Her mind was dizzy with the thoughts running through it.

How could they not have found the cabinet with the file drawer containing all those folders? She tried

convincing herself that Bray's vision might have
been off. Or that he might be a con man himself.

Only she didn't buy it.

Simon believed in Bray and his vision, so she had
to.

The cabinet and those files should have been at
the Drake offices where Heller could easily get at
them. She couldn't imagine that Heller had personal
possession of one of the antique cabinets originally
owned by Henry Drake, Brandon's grandfather and
Cliff's father.

That left only one place to search.

An option she didn't want to think about…

As they turned onto the gravel road leading to her
home, she glanced at Simon, got a glimpse of his
closed expression and could only imagine the
thoughts going through his head. She could almost
feel his roiling emotions reach out to her. Simon had
even more reason to feel let down than she had, and
Lexie sensed that his disappointment was deeper,
darker, more dangerous. He was gambling part of
himself on this mission of theirs, and he was losing.

A shiver ran through her.

Simon parked and they got out of the car without
speaking. When he took her keys, Lexie felt an
untapped energy emanate from him, leaving her
uneasy and a little breathless to see how his mood
played out. Once inside, he relocked the door and

threw the keys on a nearby table. They stripped off their outer clothing and boots.

Then, without warning, Simon pulled her to him and held her for a moment so tightly she could barely breathe. He kissed her hard and drove her backward toward the stairs. She stumbled, but he caught her, brought her down easy on a step, then came on top of her, all without taking his mouth from hers. He ripped the front of her jeans open and plunged his hand inside.

Lexie gasped. There was something different about this Simon. Something as far from soft and gentle as she could imagine. Even so, as he slid his fingers in her, never letting up on the kiss, she lit up like a bottle rocket from the inside out.

As if frenzied by her cry of pleasure, he stripped off her jeans and panties.

Wanting to know what came next, Lexie couldn't move as she watched him unzip his fly and step out of his jeans.

Then she didn't have time to think at all when he spread her legs and slid inside her, taking her like some demon was driving him. Embracing him with her legs, she thought simply to let him spend himself on her, but got caught on the wave of his passion and hung on for dear life.

Chapter Fifteen

The next morning, Lexie awoke in Simon's arms. She never wanted to leave their shelter, would spend a lifetime wrapped up in them—in him—if only fate would permit.

Truthful with herself, she was tired of going it alone, but she didn't simply want a man. She wanted *Simon*—the love of her life, her soul mate. She wanted to make a life with him. She wanted to believe he would make a good partner for her, a good father for Katie, but her doubts kept her from trusting him completely. He was used to living on the dark edge of life, which was the reason he was here in Jenkins Cove now. Could he settle down in a small town once the mystery of the human trafficking operation was resolved?

And what was his idea of resolution?

She simply didn't want to go there.

They'd spent half the night making love, but Lexie couldn't help but wonder if Simon's passion had been more to erase the frustration at hitting another brick wall than it had been due to his feelings for her.

It wasn't that she didn't believe that he cared for her. She simply didn't believe that she was the most important thing in his life at the moment. She didn't know that she—or their daughter—would ever be. Simon claimed that he wanted to see the perpetrators of the human trafficking scheme brought to justice, but she feared that he was simply driven by the need for revenge.

"Hey, you're awake," Simon said sleepily, a smile softening his face as he ran his hand down the small of her back to her naked butt.

Need immediately gripped her insides at the intimate touch; nevertheless Lexie scooted away from him and rolled out of bed.

"It's B day," she said, her heart pounding. She couldn't look at Simon, not after the thoughts that had been playing havoc with her emotions. "The Drake Foundation Christmas ball starts at six. There's still some work to be done and it's…" She checked the clock. "Good grief, it's almost ten! I need to have the fresh flowers in the truck and be at Drake House at eleven." Then it hit her. "Phil Cardon was supposed to help me finish. I don't even know if he's in jail or not."

Throughout her long-winded spiel, Simon lay

there staring at her. He kept whatever he was thinking to himself, but his smile had faded, to be replaced by a neutral expression.

"Whatever you need to do," he said.

Lexie showered in record time. This time Simon didn't even try to join her. He waited until she was dressed and scaring up a fast breakfast of coffee and toast with peanut butter and jelly—her specialty.

Then she called the police and asked if Phil had been arrested. He hadn't. Though she wasn't sure how to feel about that, she hoped Phil would show at the garden center or she would have to get someone else fast.

Simon came downstairs, his very presence making her pulse speed up.

"Breakfast," she said, in the middle of eating hers.

"Thanks. None for me."

The way he was looking at her—as if he knew what she'd been worrying about that morning—made her uneasy. She washed down the mouthful of peanut butter and jelly with a slug of coffee. A lump sat in her throat. Knowing she couldn't finish, she threw away the rest of the toast.

"We're not done, you know," he said finally. "With the key. There's still Cliff Drake's place."

The thing she'd tried to put out of mind. "You mean the Manor at Drake Acres."

"Since you say he's so competitive with Brandon,

he undoubtedly has more of the file cabinets that once belonged to his father."

Lexie knew he was right, but she hadn't wanted to think about it. "I really don't have access there, and the place is well-staffed."

Simon raised his eyebrows. "What about tonight? Won't everyone including staff be at the ball?"

"I—I suppose so. I need to be there myself, Simon. You know, in case anything needs my attention," she said, then quickly added, "My parents and my sister, Carole, and Katie will all expect me to be there with them."

Simon stared at her as if he were trying to read her mind. "You don't have to go with me this time," he said, his voice even. "I'll get in on my own."

More silence. The air was thick with things that remained unspoken between them.

Finally Lexie whispered, "I hate this!"

"What is it you hate exactly? Playing detective?"

From Simon's expression, Lexie swore he expected her to say she hated *him*.

"Thinking it could be Cliff," she said. "He's always been good to me and my family. The work he gave me saved the business a few years back. I just don't want to believe he would do something so awful. Heller has to be the one."

"I hope you're right, but I have to be sure."

"Why, Simon?" She had to get her doubts into the

open so he could ease them. "What are you going to do with the information if you find it?"

A big pause was followed by his saying, "I don't know yet."

"That's what I'm afraid of. Call Bray, have him put you in touch with his brother-in-law. We can tell him everything we know. Let the authorities handle the investigation."

"Where is this coming from?"

"From fear, Simon."

"You're afraid of me?"

"I'm afraid of what you'll do. What you won't be able to undo. It's not too late to let Detective McClellan in on what we've learned. Remember, Bray said his brother-in-law would be understanding. Maybe it's time you trusted someone other than yourself to get the job done."

"I've trusted *you*."

And now he didn't? Is that why he was so closed off, so distant?

"It's you who don't trust *me*," Simon said flatly. "Not with you. Not with our daughter. Not even with a murderer."

"I *do* want to trust you, Simon, but trust takes time, has to be earned. I don't know what you would or wouldn't do. I don't *know* you anymore," she said truthfully.

"So that's it."

His tone had a finality to it that sent a chill through her.

What did he expect of her in so short a time? After spending only three days with him, how could she know him and what he would or would not do?

"Simon—"

"Let's not argue, Lexie. You'll be late for work."

And that quickly she felt an invisible wall go up between them.

One she wasn't sure she could breach, even if she tried.

SIMON PLAYED BODYGUARD until he saw Lexie safely arrive at Drake House. Then he hightailed it out of there and headed for town.

He didn't know why he felt so let down. He'd known he was no good for Lexie, had told himself so a hundred times before he'd come face-to-face with her.

But once he had...

Wishing would get him nowhere. Nor would regret. How could he regret the time he'd spent with the woman he loved? How could he regret meeting his daughter, even if Katie didn't know he was her father?

But maybe he would have been better off.

Expecting his return to Jenkins Cove would be short-lived, especially if he found the files tonight, Simon figured he had today to make his peace with his old man, something he felt compelled to do. He could just leave without ever revealing himself, but Simon hadn't liked the way things had ended between them. And it seemed his father was a changed man.

If his father could change…

Driving straight for the Duck Blind, Simon was relieved to note that it hadn't opened for the day yet. Only one vehicle was parked in the lot, in the owner's spot.

He went inside.

The Duck Blind was a combination bar and restaurant with wood-paneled walls and a floor of wide pine planks. Tables in the center of the room were lit by lamps with fake stained-glass shades.

Rufus Shea was behind the bar, his back to Simon. Apparently sensing another presence, he turned, and when he saw Simon, he said, "It's Sunday. Sorry, but we're not open yet. You'll have to come back in an hour."

Simon took a good look at his old man. He'd aged, of course, his thinning hair and scraggly beard now threaded with gray, but he was still wearing a plaid shirt and an apron, just as he used to.

Suddenly his father's brow furrowed, the wrinkled skin around his eyes tightening. "You look familiar. Do I know you?"

Simon removed his hat. "You used to…Dad."

"S-Simon?"

Simon nodded. "I'm alive. I don't know the name of the poor kid you buried, but it wasn't me."

His father's face crumpled. Gripping the bar with both hands, Rufus lowered his head and wept, sobbing, "You're alive. My boy is alive."

Simon hadn't known what to expect, but it wasn't this. Something inside him threatened to break. He wasn't prepared. Didn't know how to handle the emotions suddenly crashing through him. So he waited until his father cried himself out and then told him an edited version of what had happened to him thirteen years before.

Rufus used a napkin to dry his tears. "I should've known it wasn't you who'd died. They wouldn't let me see your body, said better the casket remained closed. I was so sorry about the way things ended between us, boy. I was no good to anyone then. I couldn't take care of you the way a father should. I couldn't take care of myself. I'm so ashamed."

Giving into the regret he'd bottled up for years, Simon said, "Drink made you hell to live with, but you're sober now. You changed."

"I'm a different person," Rufus agreed. "I'm just sorry I didn't sober up when you needed me."

"We always need our parents," Simon told him. "That was the last straw, you know—your saying I was no son of yours. That's when I decided to run."

Rufus didn't say anything. Suddenly he couldn't meet Simon's eyes and Simon's gut quaked. What the hell?

"What is it, Dad? What aren't you telling me?"

Rufus didn't answer immediately, but finally he said, "I-I love you as much as any father could love a son." He still was averting his eyes. "You got to believe that."

"All right."

"But I wasn't able to give your mother a child… The disappointment nearly killed her. We had some problems with the marriage over it. Then she got pregnant. Not by me." Finally he looked up, locked gazes with Simon. "She never told me who he was. She said it was okay if I wanted to leave her. I didn't though. I loved her more than anything. Her death nearly killed me, too."

It was taking Simon some time to process this. "So you're *not* my father?"

"I *am* your father in every way that counts!" Rufus said. "I couldn't have loved you more, boy, since before you were born. But I was weak and jealous of your mother. I found comfort in the bottle every time I thought about her and another man, not that she catted around on me. It was just that once. She swore it, and mostly I believed her. And then when she died…"

"You forgot about me."

"I didn't forget about you, Simon. Never. Not once in the last thirteen years." More tears rolled into his beard. "I never stopped regretting denying you that last night when all you were trying to do was stop me from taking another drink. I love you, boy. I always have."

Simon couldn't help but wonder who his biological father might be, but he knew he loved Rufus Shea, no matter what. He settled down at the bar and talked with the old man until it was time for the Duck Blind to open.

Only then did he reluctantly leave, promising to be back.

His thoughts filled with the way Rufus had turned his life around, Simon wondered if it was possible for someone as damaged as he was to do the same.

Chapter Sixteen

As the sun set and the snow started falling in big fat flakes, the first of hundreds of guests arrived for the Drake Foundation charity ball, and Drake House lit up like a beautiful Christmas tree.

Having arrived early and alone, Lexie thought to keep herself busy, rearranging plants and tweaking the vases of flowers. Eventually, she acknowledged that the decorations already looked perfect and found a niche just inside the ballroom where she could see everyone as they came in.

Marie and Brandon stood together in the middle of the foyer, greeting each new arrival. Marie looked spectacular in an off-the-shoulder green velvet gown and made the perfect partner for Brandon, who could have been born in a tux. For once he was smiling. That she'd even had the smallest doubt about him made Lexie's heart twist in regret.

Shelley Zachary stood to one side, taking people's coats and handing them off to Isabella and another young woman to hang on specially set up racks just inside the private wing. Wearing what was obviously a designer black dress, Isabella looked ready to join the ball. From her expression, Lexie guessed that Cliff hadn't invited her to be his date, and Isabella wasn't at all happy playing maid tonight.

So far, a few dozen people had entered the ballroom, oohing and aahing that they'd never seen anything quite so beautiful. Lexie knew she should take more pleasure in the approval, but the Grinch was back.

She blamed Simon for her dark mood.

Oh, he'd seen to his duty as her bodyguard when she'd finished at Drake House earlier, then had followed her back here this evening. For the few hours in between he'd barely spoken to her, hadn't noticed her red silk chiffon gown with its ruched and beaded bodice and a studded bow at the hip. Indeed, he'd seemed preoccupied with his own thoughts.

Had he been making plans to break into the Manor at Drake Acres or plans to leave Jenkins Cove? Maybe both, she thought sadly.

"Lexie, there you are!"

"Mom, Dad." Lexie focused on her parents. Her mother was wearing a new deep blue cocktail dress and her father his old tuxedo. "You two look great. Where's Katie?"

"With Carole. They'll be along in a minute."

Her father kissed her cheek, saying, "My, you look glamorous."

"Thanks, Dad." She forced a grin. "Nice that *someone* noticed."

Katie and Carole entered arm in arm. Rather Carole had her arm linked with Katie's as if she were pulling her niece inside against her wishes. Apparently still miffed at being dragged from her party the night before, Katie was wearing a green dress that matched her eyes—Simon's eyes—as well as her best mulish expression.

Noticing that Katie had also worn the pendant that Lexie had given to Katie for her birthday—a gold abstract representing a mother and daughter with a square-cut emerald the color of her eyes in the middle—Lexie decided to act like nothing was wrong. She moved to the other side of her daughter, where she linked arms.

"I picked out a table for us." She indicated a large round one not far from the door. She needed to be easily found, just in case.

"It's so nice to have the whole family together outside of home or the store," her mother said.

But the whole family wasn't together. Lexie thought as they took their seats. Simon wasn't here with them and probably never would be. Their argument had crystallized things she hadn't wanted to face.

As the tables filled up with guests, Lexie looked

around the room, transformed with plants and decorations and lighting special effects. The ballroom looked like a setting in a fairy tale. Kind of like the story she'd been trying to tell herself about her and Simon.

Not wanting to spoil the evening for her family, Lexie temporarily set aside her heartbreak and concentrated on them. She checked out the buffet with her mother, who put her seal of approval on the menu. She examined the silent auction contributions with her sister, who made bids on several items. She danced with her father, who tried out new steps he'd learned in the weekly class he took with her mother. She tried to get Katie interested in anything about the ball, but her daughter was stubbornly silent, refusing to interact with anyone any more than she absolutely had to.

"You know, there are other young people here," Lexie said. "A couple of cute boys your age. They came with their parents, too. I bet you know some of them."

Katie simply sighed and did her best to look bored. Carole rolled her eyes at Lexie, who bit the inside of her lip so she wouldn't laugh. She was trying to figure out how to handle her stubborn daughter when Katie suddenly reminded her of Simon.

Feeling a little too vulnerable, Lexie excused herself and wandered over to the windows that overlooked the terrace and gardens and faced a small cove on the bay. The wind had picked up and the snow whirled and swirled in delicate patterns. On the other side of the inlet on another promontory, soft light made every window at the Manor at Drake Acres glow. Lexie felt as if she were looking out at a Christmas card.

That Simon had probably already broken in to the Christmas card seemed ludicrous to her. And frightening. How long would it take him to learn that he was wrong? she wondered.

Or that *she* was?

Just then, the band at the far end of the room stopped playing and Brandon and Marie stepped up onto the stage. Lexie hurried back to her seat at the family table.

Her daughter wasn't there.

Her pulse picking up, Lexie asked, "Where's Katie?"

"Said she had to go to the powder room," Carole whispered.

Lexie relaxed as Brandon and Marie stepped up to the microphone on a stand.

"Welcome to Drake House," Brandon said, leaning more lightly on his cane than usual. "Marie and I want to thank you all for giving your support to the Drake Foundation."

"Remember that we have some exciting items

contributed to the silent auction," Marie said, "so don't forget to put in your bid. The winners will be announced at midnight."

"Ah, winners…" Brandon said. "My Uncle Cliff has an announcement to make." He indicated that Cliff should come up to the microphone, then, with his arm around Marie's waist, left the stage.

As usual, Cliff was one of the handsomest men in the room. Certainly, he was the best dressed in a designer black tux and black silk shirt, Lexie thought, trying to push out of mind the idea that he could be a mastermind of evil. She looked around for Doug Heller, but couldn't find the operations manager among so many people.

Holding a large envelope in one hand, Cliff stepped in front of the mike. "As you know, every year the Merchants' Association sponsors a contest for the best and most tasteful holiday display. They asked me to announce this year's winner." He went on to read the list of nominations before opening the envelope. "And the winner is…Sophie Caldwell, owner of House of the Seven Gables Bed-and-Breakfast! Sophie, come on up here and say a few words."

Lexie heard the announcement as if through a filter. She couldn't help it. She barely saw Sophie's beaming face as she left the table with her niece, Chelsea, and Chelsea's fiancé, Michael, and stepped up to the mike. Though she wanted to put everything but the here and now out of mind, Lexie simply couldn't. She scanned the crowd for Doug Heller before looking back to the stage where Cliff was handing Sophie the envelope.

Staring at Cliff, she tried to see through the outer facade, tried to discern the face of evil.

If it was there, she simply didn't recognize it.

Would Simon find something to prove otherwise?

IN POSITION FOR SEVERAL HOURS, using night-vision binoculars, Simon had watched the occupants of the Manor at Drake Acres abandon it. The cars had left one at a time until none but a few high-priced toys in the main garage were left. The snow was coming down more heavily now, and it was getting more difficult to discern details. Certain that the grounds were truly empty, though, he made his run from the tree line to the redbrick buildings that comprised Cliff Drake's home.

In addition to the main house, with its three-story white pillars and the nearly-as-tall white-cased windows and balconies on each floor that overlooked the water, there were two garages—one for Cliff, the other for the servants—a guest house, a cabana and outdoor pool, and farther back from the water, the stables. At the water's edge, there was also a large boathouse and a pier jutting from it, a high-performance boat docked there despite the weather.

Did Drake Enterprises really make Cliff enough money to support such ostentatiousness? Or did a secret source of income provide him with a lifestyle most people only dreamed of? Simon guessed that the latter was more probable.

Rather than trying to breach the main house directly, he decided to approach from the rear. Overriding the security system, he didn't even need a key to open the door. He slipped inside the largest kitchen that he'd ever seen in a private home. Several doors lined the opposite wall. The first one he checked was a pantry. The second a half bath. He went straight out the third and down a hallway that led to a two-story atrium at the front of the house.

Lights were on all over the house, as if leaving him a trail of breadcrumbs to the first-floor office located off the atrium.

Once inside, he spotted the file cabinets immediately.

They were the wrong ones.

Not only were they modern, rather than antique, but the key wouldn't go into the locks.

"What the hell?"

He'd been so sure he would find the fit to the key here, but it looked as if Lexie had been correct. Then where would the damn cabinets be? What if there weren't any others?

Or…

What if he hadn't been wrong and had simply looked in the wrong room?

The manor was certainly big enough to house more than a single office. This one was situated in a high-traffic area, accessible to anyone coming in the front door. Not a good place to store valuable documents, especially not ones that could mean a prison sentence.

There had to be another office, so Simon vowed not to leave the building until he'd checked every room.

He started on the first floor and found another office, smaller than the first, but this one didn't even have file cabinets.

The second floor held a third office, but no luck there, either.

As he went through the house, Simon realized that unlike what Lexie had said about Drake House, all the furniture here was ultramodern, the artwork abstract, as if Cliff had purposely made the Manor at Drake Acres as different from Drake House as he could. Those old file cabinets simply wouldn't fit in here.

Admitting he'd run into another dead end, Simon stood in the atrium for a few moments, looking out into the snowy night. A night transformed by wind and fog like the one when he'd been taken from Jenkins Cove and thrust into a world he hadn't imagined.

An unexpected chill shot through the atrium, pebbling Simon's flesh. For a moment, he could hardly breathe.

He felt the weight of the dead on his shoulders. Of the injustice.

Felt as if myriad ghosts were pleading with him not to give up.

Looking deep into the fog curling up to the house, he could almost see them—men, women, the kid he'd seen killed. Did he really see them or was it an illusion? He blinked and when he looked again, they were gone. But the weight of their deaths wasn't. He felt it like a tangible thing, knew their souls wouldn't rest—that *he* couldn't rest—until he avenged them all.

But at what cost?

Had he already lost Lexie? She didn't trust him, but could he blame her?

He'd known from the beginning that what he'd been through had turned him into a man she wouldn't want to know. He'd lived on the edge his entire adult life, long enough that he didn't have any idea of how else to be.

His father had changed, he reminded himself. No matter that he'd learned another painful truth that afternoon, Rufus Shea would always be his old man. And if his father could choose to straighten up his life and be a man a kid could be proud of...

Shaking his head, Simon left the house the way he'd come. Only when he was about to make his way back to the road did he stop and consider the other buildings on the property. Primarily the guesthouse.

Was it really?

Suddenly an arctic cold whipped through him and he felt invisible hands pushing him, urging him toward the guesthouse. Simon acquiesced.

As he crossed the back of the property, the cold followed. His inner ghosts filled him with tension. He gazed around, on the lookout for trouble. The small hairs at the back of his neck stood up, but he saw no reason for it. He checked the ground. For as far as he could see through the snow, the fresh white cover remained undisturbed by recent footprints except for the ones he was leaving.

Only him and the ghosts, he thought, his mood darkening.

Upon reaching the guesthouse, he was surprised to find the security system unarmed. Edgy now, he tried the door handle. It turned and the door swung open. Too easy, he thought, unless there was nothing here to protect. Stepping inside, he turned on the light.

The place looked occupied, as though someone was living there. Furnished in a combination of comfortable couches and chairs and some antique wooden pieces, it had a totally different feel from the main house. The artwork was different, too—all related to the Chesapeake Bay and the Eastern Shore, from the framed watercolors on the walls to the metal sculptures of bay creatures decorating the various old end tables and a hand-carved buffet in the dining area.

Assuming that Cliff had guests for the holiday, Simon was about to leave when a cold breeze shot down his spine. He stopped and examined the room again. A briefcase lay on the coffee table. He drew closer, and saw the initials *DH* engraved on the metal clasp.

DH for Doug Heller?

The briefcase was filled with Drake Enterprises work. Why else would Heller have left it in the guesthouse if he hadn't made himself at home here?

Simon gazed around the room. Instincts buzzing, he headed for a closed door and opened it to a bedroom. A familiar canvas jacket—one he'd seen on Doug Heller—was thrown on the chair across from the bed, making Simon think the operations manager did live, or at least work, in the guesthouse.

So where were the damn file cabinets? Simon wondered as he left the bedroom.

Another door on the other side of the living area called to him. A rush of sound like wails of pain and grief unnerved him, but Simon knew it was all in his own head. He crossed to the door. His hand actually tingled as he gripped the knob. Swinging the door open, he turned on the room light to face another office.

Against the opposite wall was a file cabinet with leaf marquetry. Simon crossed the room, pulled out the key and tried the lock.

A match.

He could hardly breathe as he opened the drawer. Inside were file folders with names written across the top. Inside his head, the victims chanted their names...*Anna Bencek...Franz Dobra...Tomas Elizi...Lala Falat...*

Exactly as Bray had seen when he'd touched the key.

Simon pulled Anna Bencek's folder, which held proof of a medical check and blood workup and Anna's signed statement that she was voluntarily donating a kidney for transplant. It also held her current information—address, phone number, name and address of her shop.

The other folders gave up similar information, a folder for each transplant donor.

So Heller knew where to get to these people...

The middle drawer produced more folders with similar information. But these held information on the recipients, including who each person's donor had been and how much the recipient had paid to skip to the head of the line for a new shot at life.

Doug Heller had used his position with Drake Enterprises to run his own illegal business, and right under the nose of his employer. How had he gotten away with it all these years? Simon wondered.

Well, Heller wouldn't get away with it anymore, Simon thought as the cold seeped through him once more, straight into his bones, into his soul.

Time to mete out some justice.

Simon was so engrossed in his dark thoughts that he didn't hear the whisper of footsteps until they were practically upon him. Even as he whipped around, he heard a pop followed by an incapacitating pain.

He barely caught a glimpse of the two wires connecting to him…and then he saw nothing at all…

Chapter Seventeen

When nearly a half hour had passed and her daughter hadn't come back to the table, nor had Lexie so much as caught sight of her, she started to worry.

"I'm going to go look for Katie," she told her sister.

"She's probably with some other kids her age," Carole said. "She won't appreciate your interrupting."

An uneasy sensation in the pit of her stomach wouldn't let Lexie back down. "If she is, I'll keep walking without bothering her. I just want to make sure she's all right."

Making her way through the crowd was a feat in itself. People were shoulder to shoulder and more were arriving all the time. Lexie looked everywhere—the ballroom, the buffet, the dining room, even the upstairs parlors—but couldn't find her daughter. That uneasy sensation blossomed into something akin to panic. She began to ask people if they'd seen Katie in the last half hour, but no one had.

On her way back to alert Carole and her parents,

Lexie heard her name. Pulse fluttering, she stopped and turned to see who was calling her.

"Cliff."

His usual jovial expression was missing. "I need to talk to you."

Cliff gestured that she should follow and, not knowing what else to do, Lexie did. He crossed the foyer and passed the racks of coats into the front room of the personal wing.

Facing her, he said, "First, let me say Katie is all right."

"Katie?" Lexie's heart began to pound. "What happened to my daughter?"

"Apparently, she took herself for a walk out of here and slipped and fell on the road." Cliff patted her shoulder. "She only sprained her ankle a little, that's all. She'll be fine."

"Where is she? Upstairs?"

"No, not here. Tommy Benson found her near his place so he took her home to ice the ankle. Then he called me. He didn't have your cell number, but he knew you'd be here. I'll take you to her. Let me get our coats."

The pressure in her chest easing a bit, Lexie nodded. "Thanks, Cliff."

Tommy Benson was a Jenkins Cove police officer. Good thing he'd found Katie or she might have been out in the snow for who knew how long.

What was she doing out on the road? Rebelling against being here and going home in protest? After what Katie had pulled the night before, Lexie wouldn't doubt it. She figured she was in for a lot more worry over her daughter's escapades during the next few years.

Thinking she should let her family know what was going on, she pulled her cell phone from her purse just as Cliff came back with the coats.

"Here you are." He held out Lexie's coat for her.

She slipped her arms into it. "Thanks. I should call Carole, so she doesn't send a search party after me."

"Maybe you should wait until after you see Katie for yourself. That way they won't worry like *you're* doing right now."

"Maybe you're right."

She put her cell back in her purse. Even with Cliff's reassurance that Katie was fine, Lexie couldn't help but feel off-kilter. Knowing she wouldn't feel better until she saw Katie herself, she quickly followed him out of the house to the BMW one of the valets had already pulled up front. Cliff tipped the man who ran around to the passenger side and opened the door for Lexie.

"Try to relax," Cliff said as they fastened their seat belts. "We'll be there in a few minutes."

Lexie nodded and took a deep breath. As they set off for the Benson place, she couldn't help wishing

Simon were here with her. Sometimes it was so hard being a single parent, especially where her child's welfare was concerned.

Suddenly it hit her…Simon…at Cliff's place… In her worry for Katie, she'd forgotten about what he was doing. Surely he was done searching the Manor.

So why hadn't he called? No matter what he'd found or hadn't found, he would call to tell her about it, even if he was still angry.

Great. Now she had two people she loved to worry about.

Suddenly she realized they were slowing and she looked for Benson's house, but only saw twin redbrick pillars with wrought-iron gates decorated with a fancy *C* and *D*.

"This is the entrance to the Manor," she said, keeping her voice even, though her pulse jagged a warning. "I thought you said Katie was at Tommy Benson's place."

"I need to stop for something. It'll just take a minute." He completed the turn and started on the long drive, but he didn't stop in front of the door.

Her pulse picked up and rushed through her head so that she could hear it. "Cliff, I'm really concerned about Katie—"

"You'll see her soon enough."

But Lexie didn't think so. Had Simon been caught? Was the game up? Was that why Cliff had brought her here? Had she been wrong about him all this time?

Cliff stopped the BMW near the guesthouse. Thinking she could run, then call the police, Lexie tried the door handle.

"You won't get it open, Lexie."

"What are you doing, Cliff?" Lexie kept her voice as even as she could. The words fought her as she spoke. "Where's Katie?"

"Katie?" He opened his door and hopped out. "At the ball, I assume." Slamming the door, he walked around to the passenger side and opened her door. "Get out."

"No. Take me back, Cliff." She stiffened when he grabbed her arm. "I don't know what you think you're doing—"

Her words were cut off when he jerked her out of the car. Lexie fought him, but despite his playboy persona, Cliff was every bit as strong as Simon.

"Why are you taking me here?" Pulling against him only meant she tripped as he dragged her to the guesthouse. "What's going on, Cliff?"

"I don't have to tell you, Lexie. You already know."

Simon… Dear Lord, he'd been caught!

Suddenly breathless, she stopped fighting and stumbled after him. Once inside the guesthouse, she saw Simon in a chair facing the door. He didn't even look her way. He was slumped in his chair, hands behind his back, and his head lolled to the side. His eyes were only half-open.

Directly opposite Simon, Doug Heller held a knife as if he knew how to use it.

Feeling like a fool for believing in Cliff, she looked to him, unaffected by his regret-filled expression. "You're in on this together?"

"Not exactly."

"Old Cliffy works for me," Heller said.

"Not exactly!" Cliff repeated, this time with more emphasis.

"Oh, right. We're *business* partners. I do all the work and he takes half the money in exchange for access to his ships and yachts and properties."

So they'd done it, Lexie thought. They'd nailed the heads of the human trafficking operation.

Now the question was this: would she and Simon live long enough to tell the authorities what they'd learned?

THAT HELLER WAS TALKING so freely made Simon's gut roll. The killer wouldn't be admitting to anything unless he planned to get rid of both him and Lexie.

Not that Simon would go down without a fight. He'd stop the bastard any way he could, and if he went down with Heller, so be it. He probably deserved to die.

Why hadn't Heller killed him already?

What was he waiting for?

Heller had used a Taser on him—the reason he hadn't been able to get his hands on the man. Simon remained half-slumped in the chair, his eyes at half-mast, so Heller wouldn't realize that he was starting to recover from the powerful shock. For several minutes now, he'd been working at the knot in the rope that tied his hands behind his back, and it was starting to loosen.

"What are you going to do to us, Cliff?" Lexie asked. "Kill us?"

"The two of you pose a real problem, Lexie." Cliff shook his head. "I saved Simon's hide once, but I don't know if I can do it again."

"You saved my hide?" Simon echoed, making his voice sound unsteady, as if he were still weak from the Taser blast.

"I wouldn't let Heller kill you. I agreed to let him ship you off to be part of a paramilitary army that would keep you busy and away from here for a few years. He arranged everything."

Though he was sure he already knew, Simon asked, "Why?"

"I didn't want you to die. I figured you didn't see anything really, and by the time you came back to Jenkins Cove, any evidence would be destroyed and your memory of that night would have faded. Killing people wasn't part of the deal."

"But people did die...*Dad.*"

Cliff locked gazes with Simon. "Wh-what?"

Though he appeared shocked, he didn't deny the relationship, making Simon's gut tighten.

"Rufus and I had a heart-to-heart this morning. He spilled his guts." But Rufus hadn't known the identity of Simon's biological father, and now Simon wished he didn't know, either. "So, you couldn't kill your own flesh and blood?"

"No! I never killed anyone, Simon. I swear to you, my hands are clean."

"Clean? You knew what was going on. You made money on people's misery!"

"They wanted to come here, to live in this country. They have better lives here. They're happy—"

"Maybe those who are still alive. What about the ones who didn't make it because they didn't have the proper medical follow-up? Who died of complications, like Lala Falat? Or those who were shot to death like the kid in the woods? Or bludgeoned to death with a yachting trophy?"

"I wasn't responsible for any of that!"

"Stop whining," Heller demanded. "It doesn't suit you."

"Now I know why you've been so good to me and my family over the years," Lexie said to Cliff. "You knew Katie was your granddaughter. After all you've done for us, surely you won't let Heller kill us now."

Simon stewed inside. They *couldn't* kill Lexie
She was innocent. He'd gotten her mixed up in this
He couldn't let her pay for his sins. Even as he
thought it, the knot gave and the binding holding his
wrists together loosened. He worked one hand out
then the other.

Cliff asked, "Simon, are you willing to drop this
investigation of yours and remain silent about what
you've learned? I could make this as financially re-
warding for you as it has been for me."

Insulted that this man who was of the same blood
thought they were anything alike, Simon felt heat
creep up his neck. "No way in hell. Too many
people were harmed or killed because of you."

"All I did was rent my ships and properties to
Doug and—"

"Knock off the sanctimonious act, Cliff!" Heller
shouted. "It's not going to get you a pass."

Cliff turned on his partner. "The human trafficking operation was your idea. You ran it!"

"But if the authorities found out about us, you'd
be held equally responsible for everything that
happened."

"We won't tell," Lexie suddenly said.

Heller cocked his head and seared her with his
gaze. "Now, why don't I believe you?"

Simon didn't believe her, either. She was stalling
for time. What was she up to? Finally, his head clear

of the effects of the Taser and his hands free, though still behind him, Simon gathered himself together and waited for an opportunity to strike. Heller should have done a better job of restraining him.

His mistake.

"Really," Lexie said, inching closer to Heller. "I mean the operation is over now, right?"

"For the time being. We don't have a doctor who can do the surgeries."

Which sounded like he was planning on starting up again as soon as he found one, Simon thought. He wondered what Lexie was planning to do by getting close to Heller, who held the knife as if he was looking forward to gutting someone with it.

Too bad Heller had searched him and found the knife in his jacket, Simon thought. Too bad he had no other weapon on him other than his bare hands.

They would be enough, he vowed.

"Cliff, I'll make a deal with you," Lexie said. "I believe you when you said you never meant for anyone to be hurt. You don't have to go on letting this man use your resources. Agree to stop doing that and we'll forget everything we learned. You're my daughter's grandfather. I don't want to see you go to jail. Heller can take off, disappear to another country or something."

What the hell was she saying? Simon almost protested when she turned her attention to him.

"Cliff's your father, Simon. You don't want him in prison any more than I do, right?"

Though her words sounded like a capitulation, the tension in her expression and the denial in her eyes when she locked her gaze onto his told Simon otherwise. She was playing Cliff to get closer to Heller.

Simon's muscles coiled.

"This is bunk! Don't believe a word out of her mouth!" Heller said, charging to his feet and coming too close to Lexie for Simon's comfort.

The way he was handling the knife—like he was getting ready to use it on someone—made Simon prepare to launch himself at the bastard. But Lexie was too close. And Heller wasn't stupid. He kept a sharp eye on Simon.

"Lexie has never lied to me," Cliff argued. "She's the most honest person I know. Her child is my blood."

Simon indicated that Lexie should get out of the way. Though understanding colored her expression, she ignored him. Her eyes flashed to a nearby table.

"Then take her damn child!" Heller yelled at Cliff. "Adopt the kid. I don't care! But you're not going to let these two go. I'm not going to prison because you're a gutless wonder, as usual!"

As the men argued, Lexie reached for a heavy metal sculpture on the table—a Maryland crab.

"Watch what you say!" Cliff warned.

"Or you'll what? If you hadn't convinced me to

let your bastard live thirteen years ago, we wouldn't be in this situation!"

Lexie grabbed the crab and swung it at Heller's knife hand. The man's sixth sense must have warned him because he stepped away and the sculpture barely brushed him. While Heller's attention was diverted, Simon lunged at him and made contact, knocking him back and away from Lexie.

Heller struck out at his gut with the knife, but Simon was faster and arched away so that it missed anything vital, only slicing through the leather sleeve of his jacket and nicking his arm.

Pain seared him, but Simon was blinded with hatred and the need to make this man pay, not only for putting him on that transport ship to hell, but for threatening Lexie's life, for taking the lives of people he didn't even know.

He kicked out and made contact, knocking the knife from Heller's hand. Heller tried to go after it, but Simon tackled him. They went rolling across the floor, trading punches. Heller was heftier and definitely strong, but Simon was trained for battle and a black rage coursed through him. Rolling on top of Heller, he hit the man in the face with a series of stunning blows, then grabbed him by the throat and put pressure on his airway.

"Do you have any idea what it feels like to know you're going to die?" Simon demanded, totally focused on his enemy. He squeezed tighter so the other man was choking, trying to get air. "I do. I was certain of it day after day. I felt like I was already dead and living in hell. A place that will welcome you with open arms."

He increased the pressure on Heller's throat even more. The man's face turned red and he tried to say something, tried to pry Simon's fingers away, but he couldn't budge Simon.

"Simon, stop before you kill him!" Lexie's cry unnerved Simon just for a second. It was all Heller needed.

Heller ripped Simon's hand from his throat and knocked his arm on a nearby table. The knife wound came in contact with the table's edge and pain reverberated through Simon so that he saw stars and gasped for breath.

Heller threw him off, got up and ran straight through the open front door. By the time the pain lessened enough to allow Simon to get to his feet, the man was gone. His mind focused on only one thing, he stopped in the doorway to visually track the man's footprints, visible in the night. The snow had cleared and the moon was out. The footprints ran straight into the fog coming off the bay.

"Heller's headed toward the boathouse," he said, feeling invisible hands pushing him in that direction. He heard a silent chant in his head,

Patricia Rosemoor   257

urging him to stop Heller. "There's a speedboat docked at the pier."

"Don't go after him!" Lexie pleaded, hanging on to the back of his jacket. "What if he has a gun?"

An invisible struggle pulled Simon in two different directions. The dead wanted their justice. Lexie wanted him alive.

As he looked at the woman he loved, Simon felt the darkness and the voices in his head recede. He couldn't leave Lexie here alone with Cliff. He had to protect her.

Turning, he saw Cliff pick up something from the floor where Simon had attacked Heller. When the man straightened, his brow was furrowed. He crossed the room, holding out a delicate chain with a gold and emerald pendant.

"Wasn't Katie wearing this tonight?" he asked.

Lexie grabbed it from him. "Oh my God, Katie! Where is she?"

Simon's gut rolled. "Not here. Heller must have her." He made for the door. "He's headed for the pier."

"I'm coming with you!" Lexie said, rushing to catch up.

Cliff was right behind her, but Simon couldn't deal with the man right now, not when his daughter was in danger. He grabbed Lexie's hand and ran full-out, the chorus of ghostly voices in his head growing in urgency. They were three-quarters of the way to the boathouse when the door flashed open. Through the mists, Simon saw Heller drag Katie down the pier. She was a little spitfire, fighting him with everything she had, but she was just a kid.

His kid.

"Heller! Let go of Katie now!"

Ignoring him, Heller forced the girl into the speedboat, then jumped in beside her. Simon let go of Lexie's hand and raced for the pier so fast, his feet seemed to skim the earth as if he were about to take flight.

"Don't try to follow me and I'll let the girl live!" Heller shouted, starting the engine. "I'll even call you to tell you where to find her!"

The speedboat nearly jumped as it took off.

Simon reached the pier too late to climb aboard, but not too late to see his daughter's tear-stained, frightened face before it disappeared into the fog.

A face that would haunt his every waking moment…

Chapter Eighteen

Lexie screamed in horror as the fog swallowed her daughter, perhaps forever. For a moment, she remained frozen, her mind a void, as if she were dying.

But she wasn't dying and she refused to let Katie go without a fight. Whipping around to find Cliff coming up behind her, she shouted, "That new speedboat—the fast one—tell me it's here."

Cliff nodded and ran past her into the boathouse.

Lexie ran to Simon and as he turned to her, she saw an unfamiliar sheen in his eyes.

"Lexie, I'm sorry," Simon said. "I should have gone after that bastard Heller right away."

"You couldn't have known he'd stashed Katie in the boathouse. We'll get her back. We have to." The reassurance was as much for herself as it was for him.

"He won't let her go. She's seen his face."

Though Lexie already knew that, she couldn't lose hope. "We'll catch up to them."

"How do you think we can catch him with the

head start he has?" Simon asked, even as an engine roared to life from the boathouse.

Lexie took Simon's hand and pulled him farther along the pier, while Cliff edged the futuristic-looking craft out of the boathouse and toward them.

"That's how."

As the speedboat came alongside them, Simon leaped onto the hull then held out a hand for Lexie. She grabbed it and jumped, her stomach shaking as the boat rocked on contact. He helped her navigate the hull and climb into the seat behind Cliff, then jumped into the one next to her.

"Go!"

The speedboat practically flew into the fog. Lexie had no idea how Cliff knew where he was going or even what direction he should take as he ripped through the blinding wet cloud.

Dear Lord, let them find Katie…let them get their daughter back safely.

Lexie knew it was her fault that Katie was gone. If she hadn't distracted Simon, Heller would never have gotten away. But if she hadn't done so, Simon might have *killed* Heller. Simon had been so focused on the man, she'd feared he would do something he would regret. Killing in combat, even as a soldier in a private army, was a whole different thing from killing someone in civilian life.

Had Simon done that, he would have been held accountable. To the authorities. To her.

To himself.

For, no matter what he said about his past, Simon was truly a decent man. He had a conscience. Had he taken a life when he could have restrained Heller and handed him over to the authorities, Simon never would have rid himself of *that* ghost.

Right now, though, with Katie in danger, Lexie wondered if she hadn't made a mistake in stopping Simon. And if something happened to her daughter…Lexie could see how easily a person could get caught up in dark, dangerous thoughts like revenge.

A moment later, they tore through the fog into open water and rough seas. Through the remaining trails of mist, she could see the wake left by the other speedboat.

And then the boat itself.

Simon squeezed her hand and, tears forming in her eyes, Lexie met his gaze.

"We'll get her back," he promised.

She had to believe him. Had to believe there could be a happy ending, at least as far as Katie was concerned. Nodding, she forced down the growing lump in her throat and focused straight ahead.

Cliff guided them through the other boat's wake like it was child's play, yet the seas were rough, the ride nearly painful at times when the boat lifted into the air and then slapped down hard. Water sprayed her, but Lexie hardly noticed. She could see the people in the other speedboat now—her daughter huddled in a rear seat, Heller standing behind the wheel.

Heller kept looking back as they inched closer. Lexie could almost feel his panic increase as Cliff tried to bring their boat alongside his.

"Get as close as you can!" Simon shouted, letting go of Lexie's hand.

Simon then climbed over the front seat, over the windshield onto the hull, which rocked and bounced in the choppy seas. Even so, he stood firm, his knees slightly bent and acting like shock absorbers to his body as the boat slipped expertly alongside Heller.

Without warning, Simon leaped from the hull and Lexie's chest went tight as she stopped breathing.

HELLER'S FACE TWISTED in fury as Simon landed on the killer, the voices in his head screaming for vengeance. Heller had the advantage, however, and threw Simon off long enough to gun the boat's engine and pull it in such a tight circle away from the other craft that Simon couldn't get back up on his feet.

He threw a quick look at Katie and saw that while her eyes were swollen from crying, they were focused on Heller, and her expression was mutinous, as though she was ready to join the fray and attack the man who'd kidnapped her.

Getting her attention silently, Simon indicated that Katie should stay put, but he wasn't certain she would.

Suddenly, the engine stalled and the boat slowed and righted, allowing Simon to rise as Heller fumbled with his pocket.

When the killer pulled out a gun, Simon reacted, kicking out and hitting Heller's arm so that the gun tilted up, a shot going wild. And Simon knew that if he could, Heller would kill them all. The voices in his head urged him to stop Heller any way he could.

And he could see only one way...

Simon grabbed the other man's arm and they engaged in a bizarre dance, fighting for control of the weapon. Heller had to be stopped, no matter what it took. Instinct made him throw a quick glance at Katie, even as she rose from her seat.

"Stay there!" he yelled, finally getting hold of a pressure point in the other man's arm that allowed him to rip the gun from Heller's hand.

Simon didn't even have time to aim before Katie climbed onto the seat. As fast as she rose, Heller acted faster. With a sweep of his arm, he smacked her across the chest, tossing her off the boat. She hit the water with a scream that seared Simon's soul.

"Oh my God, Katie!" Lexie yelled.

Instinct drove Simon over the seat into the icy

water after her. At the first shock of cold, he let go of the gun. Stunned, he cleared his head and focused, then grabbed for his daughter. Tossed by the rough seas like a rag doll, she eluded him and then went under.

"Katie!" Lexie screamed again.

No, it couldn't end like this! Katie couldn't be lost to him before he even got to know her!

Simon dived down after her, blindly reaching for her, his hand brushing against her but unable to get a grip. He came up for air and went down again, deeper. This time, he couldn't find her. Couldn't see her. Panic blossomed in his chest. She couldn't die. Not Katie! Not another innocent. Another senseless death.

Gasping for air, he surfaced to an explosion of sound. Lexie was screaming their daughter's name. An engine was turning over, but not starting. The voices in his head were urging him to dive again, to rescue Katie.

He went down for a third time and thought if he couldn't find her, there was no use his coming back to the surface. He couldn't face Lexie without their daughter.

Even as he thought it, the blackness of his surroundings lifted for a moment, as if a beam of sunlight shot through the water. Or as if a ghostly mist had dived deep with him. Suddenly he was able to see a fragile hand floating as if reaching for him. A surge of strength pulsed through him and he kicked and reached out until he caught it. Tugging hard, he pulled an unconscious Katie to him.

It couldn't be too late, he thought, arm around her middle as he kicked to the surface. Cliff and Lexie were frantically looking over the side of the craft.

"You've got her!" Lexie yelled, leaning out over the water, reaching for her daughter.

Cliff reached, too. "C'mon, Simon!"

His arm hooked over her chest, Simon was careful to keep Katie's head above water as a wave rolled toward the boat. He was exhausted and shivering. The cold water held him in a death grip. Even so, he mustered enough strength to lift Katie up to her mother and grandfather. They caught the girl's arms and pulled her up and into the boat.

"Katie, honey, it's Mom!"

Cold froze Simon's limbs and sleep called him. Or was it Cliff?

"Simon, give me your damn hand!"

Cliff was hanging over the side of the boat again, arm outstretched. Simon tried reaching for it, but he couldn't do it. He had nothing left.

Then Lexie popped her head over the side of the boat. "Simon Shea, fight. Your daughter is alive because of you. *I'm* alive. We need you!"

Somehow, Simon found a kernel of strength to

reach out and grab hold of Cliff's outstretched hand. Cliff grasped him with both of his, then slowly dragged him up out of the water. Lexie grabbed hold of his jacket and with more strength than he'd known she had, helped haul him inside the boat.

Simon immediately looked to his daughter. Wrapped in her mother's coat on one of the rear seats, Katie was coughing.

Teeth chattering, he muttered, "H-Heller," then blinked and focused on the other boat. "C-can't let him g-get away."

Simon blinked again as a familiar mist hovered over the hull of the other craft. Lexie pressed into him, her hand gripping him hard as if she saw the same thing he did.

"What in the world…?" Cliff whispered as the mist took shape.

The kid he'd seen shot materialized, the apparition making Heller jump, his substantial weight whacking the side of the boat and rocking it precariously.

"What the hell!" he shouted as a large wave tossed the craft, tilting it nearly on its side.

Though Heller fought to stay upright and grab on to something—anything—he couldn't manage it. He was swept off the boat and into the water.

Simon moved to the rail, ready to grab for the killer when he came up.

Seconds passed. A minute.

"He's gone," Lexie said. "Just like that."

Simon looked up to the hull of the righted boat. Not only was Heller gone, so was the ghost.

DRESSED IN CLOTHING one of Cliff's former girl-friends had left at his place, Lexie felt uncomfortable, if dry and warm, as she sat and watched her daughter sleep in the emergency room bed. Even though Katie was safe now, the pressure in Lexie's chest had hardly diminished.

How could it when she had to see her child hooked up to all this monitoring equipment?

Needing to stretch her legs and get some air, she rose, kissed Katie's forehead and left the cubicle. She could hear Simon in the next cubicle giving his statement to Detective Rand McClellan, who'd already interviewed her.

She wanted to get home and shower and change, but she wasn't about to leave until Katie and Simon were cleared to go with her, which, according to the doctor, wouldn't be until morning. They would be monitored all night. She'd called her parents to let them and her sister know what had happened. They'd wanted to rush to her side, but she'd asked them not to come. She'd assured them that Katie would be fine and that she needed time alone to think things through.

Pacing in the hall, Lexie couldn't help but replay the nightmare in her head a dozen times.

She had to hand it to Cliff—he'd come through for them at his own expense. He'd gotten them back to land and into dry clothing while they'd awaited an ambulance. And then he'd called the state police and had turned himself in. He'd said he hadn't wanted to put the burden on her or Simon; they'd already been through enough because of him.

That she'd been wrong about Cliff deeply saddened Lexie, especially now that she knew he was Simon's biological father and Katie's grandfather.

Lexie started when she almost bumped into Detective McClellan.

"I'm done for now," he said. "I will have to talk to your daughter, as well. It can wait until she's home, though."

"Thank you. Bray said you were understanding."

"I might be, but parts of your story are going to be hard to sell the brass."

The ghost part, she knew. Not that he needed to put that in his report. A wave had tossed Heller's boat nearly on its side. Whatever he decided, Lexie would back him up and she was certain Simon would, as well.

"You'll be hearing from me, probably tomorrow afternoon. I'll give you a chance to get back home and settle in."

Lexie waited until he'd left before venturing into Simon's cubicle. Still covered with several warming blankets, he lay back in his bed, his eyes closed. She stopped to look at the face she so loved and, lump in her throat, wondered how much longer she would be seeing it.

His eyes fluttered open. "Katie?"

"She'll be fine. They just want to keep her overnight for observation. You, too."

"I'm all right."

"You're more than all right," she said softly, sitting on the edge of his bed so she could touch him. She ran her hand along his chest. "You're a hero. You saved our daughter's life."

"She wouldn't have been in danger if not for me."

"Where do you get that?" Lexie said.

"I stirred up a hornet's nest by coming back here."

"You're not guilty of anything but trying to find the truth. I'm the one who had the key. Even if you hadn't come back—"

"Don't go there."

She nodded.

"At least the souls of the dead here can rest now," he said. "And you and Katie will be safe."

"Because you'll be with us?"

He looked away from her. "I'm no good for either of you, Lexie. I wanted to kill Heller tonight."

She didn't tell him she'd felt the same when he'd tossed Katie over the side of the boat. "But you didn't."

"Because you stopped me from strangling him."

"You could have shot him once you got the gun from him, Simon, but when faced with the decision of getting revenge or saving Katie, you didn't even hesitate."

"I couldn't have done anything else."

"I know that now. I know there are things more important to you than vengeance. *People.*"

They locked gazes and Lexie wished with all her heart that she could be with Simon forever.

"I was thinking about my old man…Rufus… about how he's changed. He couldn't have done it alone. I don't know that I can, either."

"You don't have to be alone. You have me. And a daughter who will adore you. And you can get professional help if you need it, Simon, someone who knows how to deal with the kind of memories and nightmares you must have. A man can change. You proved that tonight. Please, think about staying. You have a daughter. A kid should know her father, be close to him."

"You're sure you want that?"

"Only if you do," she said, smoothing the blanket over his chest, feeling his heartbeat grow stronger. "Only if you'd be happy here. I keep worrying you'll miss the excitement and danger—"

"I've had enough danger for a lifetime. As for excitement…" He pulled her closer, wrapped his arms around her. "You're all the excitement I can stand.

I love you, Lexie, and I want to stay and get to know you all over again."

Lexie felt herself open up inside. "I love you, too, and your staying would be the best Christmas present ever."

As they kissed, she couldn't think of anything she wanted more.

Epilogue

"Da-a-ad! Stop eating the Christmas cookies or there won't be any left for our company!"

"I can't help myself. They're terrific. I'm going to expect you to keep me well fed. Your mother has lots of talent, but not in the kitchen. Do you know she tried to feed me peanut butter and jelly for breakfast?"

Entering the kitchen to see Simon pop some powdered sugar on their daughter's nose, Lexie smiled. Katie had taken to her father as if she'd just been waiting for him to show up all her life. And from the loopy grin Simon wore, it was obvious he was in love with his daughter, as well as with her.

"Hey, everyone is asking for you two," she said, grabbing a plate laden with fresh appetizers.

Simon lifted the tray of cookies and Katie grabbed bowls of chips and dip and followed her into the living area, now decorated every bit as beautifully as Drake House. The three of them had turned the living room into their own winter wonderland just that afternoon.

Now it was Christmas Eve and Lexie's parents and sister, Carole, plus Rufus, Brandon and Marie were there for the evening. Michael and Chelsea and her Aunt Sophie had stopped by for a drink.

Marie handed out flutes of champagne to the adults and some sparkling water in a flute to Katie.

"To all of us and to Jenkins Cove," Brandon toasted. "This Christmas brings us the best presents of all—love and the resolution of the terrible crimes that have haunted Jenkins Cove for years."

They all clinked glasses and Lexie sipped her champagne. How had she ever considered that Brandon had anything to do with the operation? It seemed that Ned Perry had been trying to blackmail him over a property the foundation had wanted to buy for a women's shelter. Hoping to keep the price down, Brandon hadn't wanted competitive bidding on it.

Ned had been killed because he'd overheard Doug Heller giving Hans Zanko instructions to answer the ad for survivors. Zanko had been the one to attack Lexie at her house—he'd already been arrested.

Phil Cardon had turned out to be nothing more than a petty thief who'd planned to hock Cliff's trophy.

Isabella had tried landing Cliff for herself by spying for him. She'd told him and Doug Heller about the key. Her employment had been terminated.

"I went to see Cliff this morning," Brandon said. "At his request. Simon, he asked me to tell you that he planned to sign over his share of Drake Enterprises to you."

Simon started. "I thought the government was seizing his assets."

"All but the business. Cliff inherited his half, and the other half is mine. His dirty money went into the manor and his cars and boats. At any rate, I want to continue concentrating on the Drake Foundation. I hope you'll consider taking charge of Drake Enterprises."

For once, Lexie thought, Simon seemed apprehensive.

"I don't know anything about running a company."

"I can help there," Brandon said, "until you're up and running on your own. If we don't get it together fast, a whole lot of good people will be out of work."

"Give me at least a minute to think about it," Simon said, but he hugged Lexie to him and she knew this was exactly what he needed to feel useful.

"You'll do fine, boy!" Rufus said, raising his glass to Simon.

"I heard Cliff would probably plead out to get a lesser sentence," said Michael, ever the investigative reporter. "His final actions in saving you all—and the fact that he didn't commit any of the actual murders—will be considered in his favor."

"Which means the state won't go for the death penalty," Chelsea said.

Her Aunt Sophie shook her head. "Cliff was always a brash boy, looking for attention. Who knew how far he would go to get it. At least he wasn't directly responsible for anyone's death."

"Not that it exonerates him," Marie added.

Lexie was glad Cliff wouldn't be looking at the death penalty, which would have been an added burden for Simon and now Katie. After what their daughter had been through, she and Simon had told Katie the truth about everything.

Katie had taken it all in stride like the preteen she proudly claimed to be, Lexie thought, smiling.

"Happy?" Simon murmured into her ear.

"I couldn't be happier."

Simon pulled Lexie off into the hall under the mistletoe and kissed her soundly.

When they came up for air, he said, "I never stopped loving you. I want to start my life fresh, as if the last thirteen years never happened. I promise I'll never leave if you'll make an honest man of me." With that, he pulled out a ring with a very large emerald. "I know a diamond is more traditional, but I wanted something that would remind both of us of our daughter's eyes."

Lexie held out a slightly shaking hand, but Simon steadied it and slipped the ring on her finger.

"When you agreed to stay," she said, grinning, "I thought I couldn't be happier. I was wrong." Her pulse skittered. Finally she didn't just have to dream about being happy with Simon. "I don't have nearly as spectacular a Christmas gift for you."

"You already gave me one." He looked to Katie, who shone as brightly as any ornament on the Christmas tree. "But I wouldn't mind if you gave me another one of those."

Simon kissed her again, and Lexie realized that her whole life was about to change.

She couldn't wait.

* * * * *

Silhouette Desire kicks off 2009 with
MAN OF THE MONTH,
a yearlong program featuring
incredible heroes by stellar authors.

When navy SEAL Hunter Cabot returns home
for some much-needed R & R, he discovers
he's a married man. There's just one problem:
he's never met his "bride."

Enjoy this sneak peek at Maureen Child's
AN OFFICER AND A MILLIONAIRE.
Available January 2009 from Silhouette Desire.

One

Hunter Cabot, Navy SEAL, had a healing bullet wound in his side, thirty days' leave and, apparently, a wife he'd never met.

On the drive into his hometown of Springville, California, he stopped for gas at Charlie Evans's service station. That's where the trouble started.

"Hunter! Man, it's good to see you! Margie didn't tell us you were coming home."

"Margie?" Hunter leaned back against the front fender of his black pickup truck and winced as his side gave a small twinge of pain. Silently then, he watched as the man he'd known since high school filled his tank.

Charlie grinned, shook his head and pumped gas. "Guess your wife was lookin' for a little 'alone' time with you, huh?"

"My—" Hunter couldn't even say the word. *Wife?* He didn't have a wife. "Look, Charlie…"

"Don't blame her, of course," his friend said with a wink as he finished up and put the gas cap back on. "You being gone all the time with the SEALs must be hard on the ol' love life."

He'd never had any complaints, Hunter thought, frowning at the man still talking a mile a minute. "What're you—"

"Bet Margie's anxious to see you. She told us all about that R & R trip you two took to Bali." Charlie's dark brown eyebrows lifted and wiggled.

"Charlie…"

"Hey, it's okay, you don't have to say a thing, man."

What the hell could he say? Hunter shook his head, paid for his gas and as he left, told himself Charlie was just losing it. Maybe the guy had been smelling gas fumes too long.

But as it turned out, it wasn't just Charlie. Stopped at a red light on Main Street, Hunter glanced out his window to smile at Mrs. Harker, his second-grade teacher who was now at least a hundred years old. In the middle of the crosswalk, the old lady stopped and shouted, "Hunter Cabot, you've got yourself a wonderful wife. I hope you appreciate her."

Scowling now, he only nodded at the old woman—the only teacher who'd ever scared the crap out of him. What the hell was going on here? Was everyone but him nuts?

His temper beginning to boil, he put up with a few more comments about his "wife" on the drive through town before finally pulling into the wide, circular drive leading to the Cabot mansion. Hunter didn't have a clue what was going on, but he planned to get to the bottom of it. Fast.

He grabbed his duffel bag, stalked into the house and paid no attention to the housekeeper, who ran at him, fluttering both hands. "Mr. Hunter!"

"Sorry, Sophie," he called out over his shoulder as he took the stairs two at a time. "Need a shower, then we'll talk."

He marched down the long, carpeted hallway to the rooms that were always kept ready for him. In his suite, Hunter tossed the duffel down and stopped dead. The shower in his bathroom was running. His *wife?*

Anger and curiosity boiled in his gut, creating a churning mass that had him moving forward without even thinking about it. He opened the bathroom door to a wall of steam and the sound of a woman singing—off-key. Margie, no doubt.

Well, if she was his wife…Hunter walked across the room, yanked the shower door open and stared in at a curvy, naked, temptingly wet woman.

She whirled to face him, slapping her arms across her naked body while she gave a short, terrified scream.

Hunter smiled. "Hi, honey. I'm home."

* * * * *

Be sure to look for
AN OFFICER AND A MILLIONAIRE
by USA TODAY *bestselling author*
Maureen Child.
Available January 2009
from Silhouette Desire.

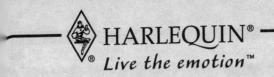

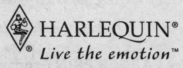

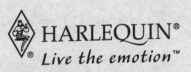

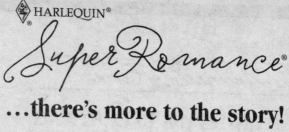
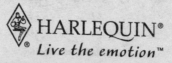

HARLEQUIN®
Presents®

The world's bestselling romance series...
The series that brings you your favorite authors,
month after month:

Helen Bianchin...Emma Darcy
Lynne Graham...Penny Jordan
Miranda Lee...Sandra Marton
Anne Mather...Carole Mortimer
Melanie Milburne...Michelle Reid

and many more talented authors!

Wealthy, powerful, gorgeous men...
Women who have feelings just like your own...
The stories you love, set in exotic, glamorous locations...

HARLEQUIN®
Presents®

Seduction and Passion Guaranteed!

HPDIR08

Harlequin® Historical
Historical Romantic Adventure!

Imagine a time of chivalrous knights and unconventional ladies, roguish rakes and impetuous heiresses, rugged cowboys and spirited frontierswomen— these rich and vivid tales will capture your imagination!

Harlequin Historical . . . they're too good to miss!